Ms Mia
and
Murder
at the
Desert Sunrise Resort

Jennifer Branch

A Grand Opening

Mia Spinel gave a last buff to an already gleaming display case. The Desert Sunrise Resort ballroom's vast parquet floor was now filled with displays of brilliantly lit exhibits. Each carefully placed treasure held a neat label, showing the historical context. A clearly marked path, outlined in multiple tape colors, would guide viewers through the exhibits.

"Everything looks good," Mia summed up. "I think we're done with the setup."

The two people next to her breathed out heartfelt sighs of relief, grateful for Mia's final sign-off on their efforts.

She continued, "Of course, we will have to clean up after the film crew finishes."

Susan Johnson, the hotel event manager, let an audible groan escape. Her face reddened in embarrassment as she mumbled, "Of course we will."

Mia completely agreed with Susan's sentiments. The last few days had been exhausting. Each exhibit contained ancient and irreplaceable artifacts, not something to trust to casual hands. Every piece was moved with excruciating care. While some of the work had been done by museum staff, most of it had been meticulously accomplished by the three of them, with the most valuable pieces finally set in place today.

As she looked around the large hotel ballroom filled with fascinating exhibits about ancient Arizona, Mia thought the past few days had been worth all the time and effort.

The centerpiece—and the whole reason for the exhibit—lay majestically in its display case at the far end of the ballroom. Visitors would slowly work their way to the culminating artifact.

Earlier this year, while excavating for a new observatory on the hotel grounds, the crew uncovered an ancient bone flute. Their construction team immediately contacted the local museum and the hotel owners. As they learned more about the flute, everyone realized how unique the flute really was.

Ancestral Pueblo wooden reed flutes had been found in Arizona, dating back well over one thousand years. They were beautiful examples of historic craftsmanship, but hardly unique. Until recently, the oldest bone flute found in North America was the L'Anse Amour flute, found all the way across the continent in Labrador and about seven thousand years old. Now, according to carbon dating, a bone flute unimaginably older—at least seventeen thousand years old—had been discovered.

Mia thought it amazing that a small item like the flute could rewrite history for the region and possibly the continent.

"We're so very lucky the construction crew knew enough to call in experts when they saw the flute," she told the museum director. "Imagine what could have happened if they were looking the other way, or too concerned about their schedule to stop work."

"Yes, it's frightening how fast a piece of human history might have been lost without their quick actions." Dr. Richard Cummings ran his hand over his close-cropped gray hair. "Not every construction crew would pause a job for an artifact." His face grew solemn, and he puffed out his round cheeks. "It's difficult to gauge how many antiquities have been lost to modern progress."

"Far too many," Mia agreed.

The hotel observatory was now under construction in a slightly altered location, still perfect for future hotel guests viewing the many stars of the Arizona night sky. This exhibit was the crowning jewel the hotel needed to publicize the Desert Sunrise Resort's soft reopening under the new Spinel Hotels ownership.

Naturally, the Spinel family decided to donate the ancient flute to the local museum. They firmly believed an important historical find should be displayed for all to see, not locked away in a private collector's hoard. However, Mia was determined to get maximum publicity for their newest hotel in the donation process. Holding the exhibit anywhere but at the hotel was not going to get them the much-needed publicity. She'd been very clear that the museum donation depended on this exhibit being hosted at this hotel, and she had gotten what she'd wanted. The museum had too.

The displays surrounding them held a combination of choice museum artifacts and fossils donated for auction. Funds would go toward displaying the important new find in its own museum wing.

Richard, the museum director, pushed his sliding glasses up his nose. "It's a lot of work for a temporary exhibit, not even at the museum. I hope it's worth it." He peered doubtfully around the room, smoothing his grizzled hair again. "I hope people bother to come all the way out here."

"I hope I've done enough promotion of the exhibit. I'm not sure we're reaching all potential visitors," Susan worried. "Maybe we should buy some more advertising? Maybe on some of the local news stations? Or add to the social media campaign?"

Her pen tapped down on her omnipresent clipboard, checking the same things off for the fifth time, Mia noticed. The wavering checkmarks overlapped in a frantic scramble, causing Mia to quietly wonder whether her events director was truly up to the job.

"It will be a wonderful fundraising event for the museum's new wing," Mia reassured them. "I personally contacted the local news, and they will be sending a crew out early tomorrow morning to highlight the event. And, Susan, you're promoting on social media already, and the museum is as well. Don't worry, plenty of people will attend. We have quite a few guest reservations for the auction night alone."

"They'll probably hide the news segment in the middle of the night," Susan said dourly. She tapped her clipboard, glaring at her list.

"Oh, I don't think they'll do that with Kyle Lee making a special Exploration Channel program all about the finding of the bone flute. It airs Friday night after he does the final filming at the exhibit tomorrow." Mia smoothed her perpetually ash blond hair with pride. It had been quite a coup getting the popular archaeologist to headline a documentary about the important new find.

The museum expert wrinkled his nose. "I can't think what the public sees in him. He's never conducted an independent dig." His long, wide nose twitched again in disgust, sending his glasses on their slow journey downward. "He's never even been published in a science journal." That was clearly the absolute bottom of the barrel as far as Dr. Richard Cummings was concerned.

"The public loves him," Mia told him firmly. "Whether he's published is not our concern."

"Oh, he's published," Richard sneered. "Popular books." Appealing to the public was clearly anathema.

"One was a bestseller, and the rest weren't far behind," Mia stated. "He'll get people in the door at the hotel and into your new museum wing after we donate the flute. That is all that matters," she said with finality. "There will be a huge crowd walking through these doors in three days, and Kyle Lee will help get them here." She continued tartly, "And those people will pay for your new museum wing."

Richard looked mutinous, but he wisely kept his mouth shut. Mia could see him thinking that the Spinels' flute hadn't been donated quite yet.

"I hope we've allowed enough parking. And crowd control." Susan effortlessly moved to a new worry. "With the hotel's soft reopening, we really don't have everything organized yet. There's so much construction going on still." She pursed her lips, smearing her lipstick.

Mia noticed, besides its inexpert application, the orange color clashed horribly with Susan's skin tone. She inwardly sighed and repeated, "It will be fine." She smiled at them reassuringly. "Now, would you two lovely people like to join me for dinner at Mesquite tonight?" As Richard visibly hesitated, she added, "The Wallaces will be there."

All hesitation fled. "I'll be there." Susan nodded in agreement, also.

"Eight o'clock," Mia told him, inwardly smiling. The Wallaces were huge museum donors. There was no way the museum director—or the hotel event organizer—would miss a chance for a dinner with them, no matter how tired they were. She wondered how Richard would react to the news that Kyle Lee would be there as well. She decided to let that be a surprise. Why have him upset beforehand?

Giving one last look around the exhibit room, Mia locked the door. Frowning slightly at the antiquated security keypad, she resolved to have another little chat with the hotel manager. Nodding to the young concierge, Atsa, who gave her a cheerful smile as she continued helping a guest, Mia knocked briefly on the manager's door and opened it.

Don Lagarto straightened up in his chair, blinking slowly in evident confusion. He was so fat he seemed rooted to his chair, like an overgrown cushion. His oily skin glistened in the dim light, and he rubbed his eyes, resembling a massive baby.

Mia chose to ignore his obvious nap. "I just finished the exhibit installation. The extra security system I ordered has not been installed yet."

"Yes, yes," he agreed. He made no further explanation.

She waited a moment in silence, then asked directly, "Can you tell me why the security system hasn't been installed yet? You told me they were installing it today. You told my son it was last week. When exactly is the security system scheduled for installation?"

He shrugged his thick shoulders, sending jelly-like ripples across his mountainous fat. "They wanted too much money. I told them no."

"They wanted too much money?" Mia repeated after him, very slowly.

He shrugged again. "Too much. I told them to go cheat someone else," he concluded with smug pride.

Mia waited a moment, then carefully said, "We have millions of dollars in fossils and other artifacts in the exhibit hall right now. Millions. We are responsible for those artifacts while they're in our hotel. Our insurance insisted on the new security." She glared, "And you tell me they wanted too much money to install the security I'd agreed on?"

He lazily held out his hands to calm her. "Hey, relax, Mia. No one wants to steal some old, broken pottery and rocks. Nothing to worry about." His puffy eyelids drooped a little.

"Give me the quote," Mia said through clenched teeth. She held out a commanding hand.

Don started scrabbling around on his desk in a disorganized pile of papers and fast food wrappers. Mia watched in horror as he overturned a coffee cup onto everything, blotted it slightly with his tie, and continued distributing the spill around his desk. She realized she didn't want to touch anything from his desk.

"Never mind," she told him.

He stopped immediately, blinking lazily in the dust motes he'd stirred up.

"What security do you have on the resort team?"

"We have Chester and the guys under him," he said, after he'd thought a minute. He told her, "Of course, we hire extras for big events. But that hasn't happened in a while. Nothing much happens around here. Quiet hotel—no need for extra security."

"Mr. Lagarto, will you please get it through

your head that this exhibit is a huge event for the hotel. There will be many more such events happening. The hotel is under new ownership. The Desert Sunrise Resort is now a Spinel Property, and everything that happens here reflects on Spinel Hotels," Mia said coldly. "A theft at this exhibit, especially when we do not have the agreed-upon security system, would cost us millions, as well as be terrible publicity, instead of a grand reopening."

"No one's going to steal rocks. Not around here. The desert is full of them—that sounds like a big city problem. Don't worry about it." He shifted in his chair uncomfortably. His eyes caught hers briefly before they flickered away.

"Someone will steal anything if other people will pay for it," Mia kept her voice very calm, despite an intense desire to yell at the manager. "As I have told you repeatedly, for an exhibit this important, we must have the best security. That is why I am here, at the last minute, to make sure the exhibit and your security are ready." She took a deep breath. "It's clearly not."

"No one's going to steal a bunch of rocks," he repeated his mantra.

"Mr. Lagarto, you will immediately call in all available security for tonight. That means everyone on the security team and anyone else you can get. Hire a local security company for the next two weeks to supplement your resort team, as I previously requested. You will station them in and around the exhibit hall. I want at least five security guards guarding that room by this evening." She looked down at him, and he squirmed in his chair. "Will you do that immediately?"

"Yeah, I'll do it when I have a chance," he said, not meeting her eyes. "Of course, I'm not going to be responsible for the extra cost to the hotel for guarding rocks."

Mia spoke over his excuses. "I will call back the security company and pay whatever exorbitant cost they charge us after you," she looked hard at him, "cancelled my order. Hopefully, they can install it before the Preview Party on Friday night."

"That's not my fault," he blustered. "I've been the manager here forever. I know what we need and what people are just trying to scam us on. I'm not paying extra for security we don't need."

She just stared at him.

He blinked slowly and looked away. "Our security is fine," he told her.

"Call all the security you can get." When he still looked mutinous, Mia repeated, "Call them immediately. That's an order." She left, shutting the door very softly behind her.

She waited to call Mark, her stepson and CEO of Spinel Hotels, until she reached her cottage. "Mark, your instincts were absolutely right on the manager here. He is worthless."

A soft chuckle, "Would an 'I told you so' be in order?"

"Absolutely." Mia gracefully collapsed into a soft chair, looking out the window. "The man is a fool. He actually cancelled the new security system, after telling me yesterday they were installing it today."

"He what?" She heard his chair come down with a thump. "We don't have security on the museum exhibits? Do you know how much money those exhibits are worth? What do you mean, no security system?"

"No security worth anything. All those valuable fossils on display, and I could probably pick the lock with a hairpin," she stated flatly. "I've made arrangements for guards tonight."

"Good," with a note of relief.

"With the manager."

A flat silence.

"I wondered if someone at the main office could call the security company and make sure that's set up as soon as possible?" She explained, "I would do it myself, but I have dinner plans tonight. And somehow I doubt Mr. Lagarto will get around to it with his busy nap schedule. If they have security guards available, they should send them as well. I'm not confident in Mr. Lagarto setting that up either."

"No problem," Mark agreed. "And I'll be arranging for Mr. Lagarto's replacement ASAP as well. He didn't seem ideal, but the hotel numbers were quite strong—a solid profit margin, considering the condition it was in. I was trying to leave as many of the old management in place as possible to smooth the transition, however," he trailed off.

"He's certainly not up to Spinel standards," Mia sniffed.

"Anything interesting for dinner plans?" Mark asked.

"Not really. Some big museum donors, the museum director, and our event planner. Oh, and Kyle Lee, the expert archaeologist doing the program on the fossil. It will give me an opportunity to check out the Mesquite Restaurant. From everything I've heard, it's fabulous."

"You haven't eaten there yet?" Mark asked in mild surprise. "That doesn't sound like you."

"No, I've been too busy to appreciate the dining experience. They brought me a lovely dinner last night, but I've been working the entire time."

"I didn't realize things were that bad. I thought you'd just be polishing a few rough edges," Mark sounded concerned.

"The exhibit was more of a mess than you thought. But don't worry, I have it all straightened out and looking fantastic. It will be an asset to our renovated hotel and a perfect reopening."

"I never doubted you'd make the exhibit a success." Mark chuckled. "But it's a huge problem having no security system in place for an exhibit that valuable. I've been concerned since our people spotted those online posts from a thief trying to presell the bone flute and other fossils, before he even stole them." His voice rose in anger, "From us. At our hotel. It could cost us millions. And you're telling me there's no security?"

"I know, Mark. That's why I'm here," Mia reassured her stepson.

There was a brief silence. "Speaking of rough edges, how is Sam doing?" Her nephew was doing a gap year working at the hotel, starting at the bottom and hopefully working his way up. There was nothing like real-world experience to find out what type of job you were most suited for.

"Sam joined me for dinner in my cottage last night. He seems to really be enjoying the work experience," Mia told Mark. "He's made it up to waiter, so far," she said with pride. "I'm looking forward to hearing him play tonight. He said he'd be at Mesquite."

Mark chuckled. "I'd wait until you hear it first. Remember Christmas."

"I'm sure he'll be fine." Sam played guitar in the hotel restaurants in the evenings to make a little extra money.

Mia stood up as she put down her phone, gazing around the room. The small adobe casita felt cool and calm in the golden evening, with warm ochre walls and a wood-beamed ceiling. Woven rugs splashed bright reds and oranges on the otherwise serene peace of the room. A small, rounded fireplace, a kiva made of clay, sat ready to be lit in the evening chill. She looked forward to curling up with a good book in front of a roaring fire after the exhibit was launched.

Tall French doors looked toward the high desert. The distant mountains were fading to rich purple, with bright green cacti dotting the rust-red of the desert.

Pouring herself a sparkling glass of champagne from the temptingly icy bottle sitting ready, Mia pushed open the door into the beautiful view from her small patio. A comfortable chair and table waited. She sat sipping the crisp bite of the dry champagne and watching the purples of the mountains streaking with sunset orange, the mountain range gradually enveloped by the deep blues of dusk.

Tiny stars flickered into lights in the velvet dark sky. She sighed in contentment. The night sky in Arizona was lovely beyond belief, tiny points of starlight sparkling to infinity.

A little reluctantly, she left the starlit night and went inside to change for dinner. Soft, warm lighting gave a welcoming glow to the small cottage's interior. A peaceful, cozy atmosphere enveloped her, and she smiled in anticipation as she got ready for her little dinner party.

Mia dressed in a soft blush pink that would coordinate well with the warm ochres of the dining room. A sheer silk scarf in deep, undulating reds wrapped her neck, adding a dash of rich color. She smiled at herself in the mirror as she added the final touch of sparkling pink spinel earrings—given by her husband on their tenth anniversary in Venice—and dark rose pink lipstick. It was going to be a wonderful night.

The crisp night air felt pleasant during the short walk to the main hotel from her cottage. The cottages lined the outskirts of the main hotel grounds, since most guests who desired a cottage also wanted privacy. Paths were well lit, but a little more glaring than she liked since the bright light veiled the soft beauty of the night and hid the stars. However, she knew the local rattlesnake population was numerous and decidedly did not confine their activities to daytime. Mia had absolutely no desire to encounter a snake on her way to dinner.

The winding path led through some of the citrus grove the hotel cultivated for their restaurant. She breathed in the honey-sweet fragrance of the citrus blossoms lying heavy in the night air.

The Desert Sunrise Resort was the first Spinel hotel in the desert. The Spinels' hotel chain had hotels on the ocean, perched in rainforests, and nestled on the side of mountains, even a few luxurious small establishments in cities. The almost flat plain of the desert, abruptly ending in the high mountains, felt very different from their other hotel landscapes, Mia thought. This mountain range wasn't particularly large for the area, but its vast bulk overshadowed the hotel and grounds. There was something awe-inspiring about looking directly up into the mountains.

The low hotel sprawled over several acres, blending into the scrub of the desert with ochre adobe walls. A few splashes of bright greens, like the citrus grove, restaurant garden, and swimming pools' landscaping made an oasis in the warm desert sand. Mia appreciated how the hotel complemented its environment so perfectly.

The Spinels' renovations were still ongoing in the outbuildings, but mostly finished in the main buildings. They had modernized the amenities and repaired structural defects, but kept the essential character of the hotel. This was Mia's first trip to the hotel, and she absolutely loved it.

Flickering oil lamps in wrought iron holders lit the main hotel entrance, transporting you back to a more leisurely era. Intricately carved wooden doors opened onto the cool desert night. A fire cheerfully danced in the rounded fireplace, with a few couples grouped around the flames. Massive hewn beams held up the high ceiling, with a balcony edging a second level in the rafters. When Mia looked up, she saw groups chatting at the edge of the high wooden rails, looking down to observe and gossip about newcomers. She smiled up at them and planned some quiet time in that optimal vantage point.

Dinner tonight was a treat she'd been anticipating. The three-star hotel restaurant, Mesquite, was one of the major reasons the Spinels had bought the property. The resort was a little off the beaten track, but the amazing restaurant drew people from all over the area for a spectacular dinner. The less than ideal hotel upkeep did not always convince them to spend the night, but she thought that could easily be changed with their renovations.

And a change of manager. Don Lagarto was clearly not responsible for the success of the restaurant. He was much too fat to fully appreciate food. She looked forward to meeting the head chef who had created the premier restaurant.

Mia had only waited a few minutes when she saw Estela Wallace hypnotically swaying across the lobby. Her huge brown eyes and full red lips were overshadowed by her curving figure. Every male eye immediately tracked her as soon as she entered, her small, voluptuous frame carefully guarded by her protective husband. Women's eyes followed her path sourly, realizing they had been neatly eclipsed.

Hands outstretched, Estela enthusiastically embraced Mia, with a loud kiss on each cheek. "Mia, darling, thank you so much for inviting us tonight. I can not wait for your lovely party on Friday! And John is so excited to see the flute!" She stage whispered, "He still hopes you will sell it to him, but I tell him you never will." Her ruby lips curved in laughter.

John Wallace shook hands briefly, while his vibrant young wife chattered on. "Mia," he acknowledged, then motioned a waiter for a drink.

Mia liked the Wallaces. They had been extremely easy to work with in both the details of the fossils they had loaned for the exhibit and several that they had donated to the charity auction. The only small difficulty was that John Wallace desperately wanted the bone flute for his own collection. The sums he'd offered for it so far had been extremely tempting to anyone who didn't view it as a national treasure.

John Wallace seemed pure vintage Texas oil man, with a big silver belt buckle and elaborately worked but well broken-in cowboy boots. He held a bourbon in his big hand, as usual, but it never seemed to affect him much. Over his lifetime, he'd amassed the largest private collection in the world of Southwestern fossils and historic artifacts.

Estela Wallace was a much more exotic creature, attracting male eyes wherever she went. Her large eyes slanted mysteriously, helped along with expertly applied winged eyeliner. Her reddened full lips were an invitation to male eyes, and her lush figure a perfect hourglass with curves in all the right places. She was very much younger than her very rich and obviously smitten husband. Most people made the obvious assumption. Mia wasn't so sure.

Estela looked up through her long lashes at her husband, who neatly tucked her under one arm. He bluntly asked, "How about a sneak preview of the exhibit, Mia?"

"Now, John, you know I can't do that."

"I'd make it worth your while. You know that."

"Now, John, if I let you in, everyone else will want to come too. We just finished organizing it today."

"Anything good?"

"The pieces you lent are, of course. And I know the museum appreciates your very generous silent auction donations."

"Yeah, but is there anything I might want in that silent auction?"

Mia considered, "I think there might be a few pieces that will pique your interest." She hedged, "I'm not certain of everything you have in your collection already, of course, but there are a few quite special ones."

"Good enough odds for me. What do you think, honey?"

Estela looked up through darkened lashes and smiled at him, "I think you will be sure to find something. You always do, especially for a good cause as well."

"True enough."

"And tomorrow you will go riding with me. I want to see where the flute was found and if there is anything else there." She smiled at Mia, "The whole story is like something out of a movie, an adventure." She smiled in a slow, beautiful curve. "Treasure hunting."

"I don't think you'll find anything else, but you're welcome to try," Mia told her.

Estela pouted slightly in disappointment, then shrugged elaborately. "Still, one never knows."

"No, anything might happen. That's the fun of it," Mia laughed. "It's a beautiful trail ride, I'm told. You might take a picnic lunch with you. I'm told Mesquite packs an excellent one."

"Good. If I have food, then John will come too," Estela stated.

"Honey, I'd follow you anywhere." John grinned at her like he meant every word, a man looking at the woman he loved.

"I would too, Estela darling," a professionally smooth voice cut in, and a handsome man leaned forward to kiss her on the cheek, lips lingering a beat too long. "It's been far too long. How's your father?"

Mia saw Estela stiffen slightly, visibly forcing herself to keep a social smile. "Kyle, how unexpected. I didn't know you were coming tonight."

Kyle smiled archly at her. "I know you didn't, darling. What a lovely surprise for you, isn't it?"

John grunted, "Kyle." He took a gulp of his bourbon, draining the glass, and handed it off to a waiter. "Another."

"John," Kyle parried, then smiled winningly at Mia, "You're looking lovely, Mia darling."

Mia nodded, "Hello, Kyle." She wondered what the well-known archaeologist had done to annoy the Wallaces. "Are you ready for the program finale?"

"I finish filming tomorrow," he said impressively. "You can come see the filming as my very special guest." Kyle's smile showed every single one of his pearly white teeth. He was dressed impeccably in a pale tropic-weight suit with a carefully knotted striped tie and crisp white shirt. He looked like a sleek, elegant cat dressed up for the evening.

"That sounds interesting." Mia planned to drop by the filming to make sure everything was going smoothly.

Susan Johnson and Richard Campbell came in together, clearly still discussing the exhibit details. Spotting the others, they joined the little group.

Susan had evidently dressed in the dark with a black top and navy slacks that didn't match as well as she'd probably thought they did. Mia thought the combination looked like a bruise. Her hair was scraped back from her forehead and confined with a dollar-store rhinestone clip, already sliding down her hair. She smiled dutifully at everyone, then hunched her shoulders to avoid conversation, ducking her head down, like a retreating turtle.

Mia sighed inwardly at the lack of confidence and sense of style. And the girl probably thought she was being dressy with the cheap sparkles, which no one could pull off without confidence. Youth wasted so much time in that awkward stage.

Estela barely flickered her long lashes at Susan, seeing no competition from that quarter.

Richard, wearing a poorly tailored funeral suit, bagged at the knees and bulged elsewhere. He purposefully held his hand out to John. "John, a pleasure to see you and your lovely wife." He smiled briefly at Estela, unmoved by her allure, then purposefully turned back to John. "Susan and I were just going over some of the last-minute details for the exhibit."

Glancing at Mia, he said optimistically, "I had a little idea about the exhibit. I think we might move the main exhibit over to the North side of the room. Create a little more anticipation." He rubbed soft fingers together, excited about the change.

Mia sighed to herself. Richard's little ideas were one of the reasons the past days had seemed interminable. She kept her voice even, "Richard, that would change the entire traffic flow of the room. We need to leave it how it is. It's going to be difficult enough to get it ready on time after they finish filming."

Kyle broke in, "What about moving the bone flute to the other side of the room, next to the windows? The sunlight streaming down on it would make great footage."

John said shortly, "Sun exposure would fade the coloration."

Kyle looked like he might argue, but Richard

broke in, "John's right, Kyle. Sunlight is the last thing we need on that artifact."

Mia said more cheerfully than she felt, "So that's settled. We'll just keep the exhibit exactly as it is."

Richard set his pudgy jaw defiantly, but said nothing.

Susan looked like she missed crossing that item off her clipboard.

"And welcome the crowds. Everyone will love it," Estella ably seconded Mia. "Now, let's go see what amazing creations your chef has made for us tonight." With the complete assurance of the belle of the ball, she walked toward the restaurant doors, admiring glances following.

The headwaiter quickly opened the big doors, discreetly informing her, "Ms. Mia, I have a quiet table ready for your party on the far side of the room." He led her to a table situated in a corner with a clear view of the long, low room. For the first time, Mia wondered how old the main building actually was. Was her modern resort built around an ancient ranch or something even older?

As she passed the guitarist softly strumming in the corner, he gave her a huge wink and briefly played a fanfare. She firmly shook her head at him, and he grinned back unrepentantly. Sam, her nephew, was the dinner musician tonight, as promised.

"Thank you, Tahoma," Mia said. The headwaiter himself had brought Sam's and her late dinner to her cottage last night, and they'd chatted for a few minutes. They had very similar ideas on what made meals great.

Without asking her, he'd readied a chilled bottle of champagne of her favorite vintage. "Champagne?"

Everyone settled into their chairs, smiling at the bubbly glasses. John swirled the refill of his bourbon, glowering into the amber liquid. The light gleamed on the face of his leather-strapped Breitling Navitimer. He'd sat as far away from Kyle Lee as possible, pulling out a chair for his wife to sit beside him.

The low ceiling was intricately carved and painted, making their corner of the large room seem intimate. Sam played soft guitar music, a soothing background to conversation. Heavy oak tables with rust linen tablecloths held flickering candle lights, and gas-lit torches hung on the walls, creating an intimate oasis of light around each table.

Kyle raised his glass, smoothly preempting the first toast, "To the upcoming exhibit and my program."

They all sipped to the shared goal, and the mood relaxed. "Now, what do you have for us tonight, Tahoma?"

"Tonight, we have bison steaks grown on the ranch next to the hotel, accompanied by a spicy smoky aioli, new potatoes, and fire-roasted peppers sourced from the hotel garden. Chef Chooli makes fabulous stone-ground corn tortillas." He smiled benevolently at the group. "I would suggest some smoked trout dip and tortillas as a starter."

"That sounds delicious," Mia agreed.

"We also have fresh-caught trout from the mountains, with spicy pepper salsa."

Estela ordered a bison steak. "Mmm, wonderful."

Mia followed her lead. It was nice to be at the hotel long enough to try everything. Going to a fabulous restaurant only one time made choices much more difficult. She knew she would be back for that trout.

Richard returned doggedly to his attack on Kyle. "Now, Kyle, if you'd gotten your Ph.D, like me, you'd realize sunlight is almost the most harmful thing in a museum to a delicate artifact. The last thing we want is the flute breaking down in sunlight." His cheeks puffed in prideful disdain.

Kyle showed every sharp white tooth as he replied. "Naturally, I realize that, Richard. In my last best-selling book — you may have noticed it made the New York Times' bestsellers list — I made that exact point. I simply did not realize the windows would be open during the exhibit. A few brief moments for filming would make no difference." He turned to Mia, "Aren't the windows rather a security risk?"

John put in, "We haven't gone into your security in detail, Mia. What do you have?"

Absolutely nothing at all, Mia thought sourly to herself, but said reassuringly, "I have a guard team, both hotel and extra security, overseeing the exhibit tonight. They should install the final exhibit security tomorrow, after Kyle's filming in the morning." She smiled at Kyle, "We didn't want to have the security system filmed or be in the way of filming." That made a plausible explanation, she thought.

John nodded with a slight frown, turning his glass on the table thoughtfully, watching the water ring enlarge on the rust colored linen.

"Tomorrow, after filming?" Kyle frowned. "That doesn't give much time to install it. And what if we need retakes?" He took a long drink of his iced tea.

"Aren't you just saying a few words about the flute and other artifacts?" Richard asked. "Besides putting on your makeup, don't you have about ten minutes in front of the camera, at the most? It's not like you have to actually write anything yourself—your writer did that already. And you've already filmed the rest of it, right? Should be quick, even if you mess up some." He took a sip of deep red wine, snickering into his glass.

Before Kyle could answer, Mia said, "The film crew has the exhibit hall to themselves for the entire morning. That should be ample time." She smiled at Kyle, "I know all kinds of things must come up during filming. We all want an engaging documentary that brings people to the exhibit."

Estela nodded in rapid agreement. "We want everyone to know about it. The more people know, the more people come." She looked around the table brightly, smoothing her rich dark hair into place, her ruby red dress making her brown eyes impossibly luminous in the candlelight. "The more people come, the more people spend money, and the museum is happy." She smiled at Richard, "Then, he stops asking us for money for his new wing, because it is already funded."

Richard smiled back sourly at her.

"Now, tomorrow, I ride out to the dig site. We have such experts here; tell me a little more about it." Her eyes danced with the lure of buried treasures not yet uncovered.

Richard cleared his throat importantly, but Kyle slipped in first. "The archaeologists finished working there a few weeks ago, when we filmed the site. None of their other finds have been spectacular. Mostly pottery shards, some seeds, which we carbon-dated to confirm the flute's age." Kyle swirled the champagne in his glass, watching the bubbles fizz and pop between his long fingers.

Mia had actually been relieved when they found no other important discoveries. Too many interesting finds, and the government would start dictating how the hotel's property was used. Allowing the university to dig was a compromise that had thankfully ended well for all.

Personally, she rather enjoyed the pottery shards. The little fragments offered glimpses into the everyday life of a long-ago people. People who made meals and stored bountiful harvests, just as people do today.

"Maybe we'll spot something ourselves, honey," John said, with a dreamy tone in his voice. He quickly nodded to Mia, "Naturally, anything we find we'll report to you."

"Yes, you report all your finds to the proper

authorities, don't you, John?" Kyle laughed softly under his breath, tossing back his champagne glass. "Of course you do." He motioned for a waiter for more iced tea.

John's lips pulled back from his teeth, but it was not in a smile. His hand gripped his glass harder. Mia saw Estela pat his hand under the table, calming him down.

With a flourish, Tahoma set down appetizing tastings of smoked fish, steaming tortillas, and charred pepper salsa at their places. Mia took a bite of the tortilla and smoked trout. It was amazing, the smokiness of the fish just enough to enhance the flavor, the tortilla with its rich depth of corn, the spicy warmth of the peppers. She smiled at Tahoma in approval. He went away beaming.

"I do hope the security will be finished by Friday morning. We want the preview party to go well, not have workmen all over the place while we're setting up." Susan fussed, tearing up her tortilla into her salsa. "There's just so much to do before the party. And after that, so many people were going through the exhibit." Her hair straggled down in untidy clumps.

"I'm sure they'll finish everything they need to do," Mia reassured her.

"It would just be so awkward if a bunch of security people were wandering around while we're setting up the event," Susan balled up her napkin, then smoothed it out. "Everything needs to go perfectly."

Mia wondered how many events Susan could possibly have managed if she expected everything to go perfectly. The whole point of an event manager was to prepare for all of the things that could, and probably would, go wrong, so that the guests never even knew about them. "I'm sure it will be fine," she told Susan again.

"I've actually had a fire in the bathroom at one exhibit opening I spoke at. Smoke poured into the exhibit hall. Everyone was coughing like crazy, and the sprinklers went off. We had to evacuate in the rain." Kyle's contribution was hardly designed to help calm Susan. She dropped her napkin and awkwardly leaned under the table to retrieve it.

Kyle continued, his dark eyes gleeful, "And at another one, the centerpiece of the exhibit was stolen on opening night. Swiped from under all of our noses." He looked around the table with a smirk on his face, seemingly delighted with the expression on Susan's face. John stared back at him stonily.

Richard said, his disapproval clear, "It's not like you've had anything to do with the exhibit organization here, Kyle. You're just filming it." He pushed his glasses up, peering at Kyle through them. "I've never had that kind of problem at any of my exhibits. They sound extremely poorly run. Did you organize those?"

The conversation was awkward, to say the least, with all three men actively sniping at each other. Slogging determinedly through the conversation, Mia finally saw their feast coming. Steaming trays filled with delicious food were always a welcome distraction. The table calmed as everyone ate the star chef's meal and listened to the soft guitar strumming. She sipped the aged Tempranillo Tahoma had paired the main course with, and felt herself relaxing into the evening.

Looking around the long room, Mia noticed a family with two well-behaved children, both boys. It was unusual to see children in a main dining room in the evening, reminding Mia of taking her boys to the family hotels and out to dinner during vacations. They were the only family group in the room. She smiled at the children's appreciation of the food—it disappeared at a rate she hadn't seen since her own boys were small.

Mia noticed that even though the room didn't feel crowded, there were no empty tables, always a sight that warmed the owner's heart. The restaurant seemed very well run.

Tahoma, clearly an excellent headwaiter, had thoughtfully seated couples in the most romantic, intimate niches, leaving the less private central area to larger parties. Everyone seemed to be enjoying themselves.

A wiry man reached high above his head, miming what must be today's rock climb. His equally athletic companion smiled good-naturedly at him, clearly remembering a shorter distance than he did. Mia noticed one young couple with shiny new wedding rings, clinking glasses, and gazing lovingly into each other's eyes.

Many of the other guests were older women, some relaxing alone, and a few groups having spa weekends. A mother and daughter laughed at a shared joke, faces glowing from their spa treatment and the evening.

A thin man dined alone in a niche, a huge book propped up against the table's heavy iron candlestick, risking a fire with each page turn. Mia noticed a waiter hovering attentively by with a large water carafe. She squinted a little; the book's cover showed a hovering spacecraft and proclaimed to know the secrets behind UFOs. She smiled a little at the reader's intense expression, notebook and pen at the ready. A true believer, then.

A woman tripped, nimbly caught by Tacoma. She hurried to meet another woman waiting impatiently at a window table, frowning at the menu. The woman dismissed the other's fervent apologies for her tardiness with an impatient wave, hampered slightly by several strings of her turquoise beads clattering against the table. The tardy guest perched on the edge of her chair, clearly unsure what and when to order. Flitting through her menu, she hesitated at choosing anything, instead looking around the room in curiosity. Her host finally snapped her menu shut with a frustrated look, imperiously motioning the waiter over to order for both diners. She clearly hadn't found what she was looking for in the menu, but was determined that they would get it.

Mia wondered what the woman could possibly want that wasn't on the menu. She always considered the opportunity to try local specialties one of the best parts of travel. You never knew what wonderful new dish you might enjoy if you were open to new possibilities.

The food was absolutely delicious, the bison

steak perfect in texture, the aioli just hinting of exotic spices, and the Tempranillo wine deep in rich notes of leather, blackberry, and tobacco. The table was quiet in appreciation. They peacefully discussed the hotel plans, including the new observatory, and some of the more interesting upcoming workshops Susan had scheduled.

Dessert was classic flan done right, with a honey orange sauce "from the hotel orange groves," Tahoma told them with pride. Delicious.

As soon as he finished his dessert and drained his iced tea, Kyle looked around the table with a satisfied smile. "Mia, you were an absolute darling to invite me to dinner. I've enjoyed it immensely, but," his full lips made a mock pout of distress, "I need to hit the hay. Filming tomorrow, you know. I have to get my beauty sleep."

"I completely understand. It was good to see you, Kyle," Mia said.

"Richard, John," he nodded shortly at the men. He came around to Estela and held out his hand, kissing her delicate fingers when she tried to politely shake hands, "My lovely Estela."

John's chair made a slight scraping sound on the tile floor.

With seeming reluctance, Kyle let Estela's hand go and said, "Goodbye, all." He blew another air kiss at Estela, who was looking down at her dessert plate, studiously ignoring him. He didn't waste one of his brilliant smiles on Susan. Women turned to watch him stride away with his air of complete assurance. Mia smiled as she noticed both women at the table by the window turn completely around to watch Kyle's confident figure leave.

"And good riddance," John muttered. Richard clearly agreed, scooping up another bite of flan with gusto.

The atmosphere around the table relaxed after Kyle left. Good food and good wine always had that effect, Mia thought with a smile. Even Susan calmed down her worrying somewhat, though she still looked a little lost without her clipboard.

The family with young boys had appropriately left early, but Mia noticed the newlyweds lingering at their table, holding hands and gazing at each other as they sipped their wine. The woman with the turquoise beads—and an equally hampering, voluminous handwoven skirt—stayed deep in conversation to her companion while almost bolting her delicious meal. Gesturing around the dining room officiously, she almost caught her floating bell sleeves on fire several times in her sweeping gestures. The other woman toyed with her food uneaten, while earnestly listening and cautiously offering encouragement to the informative talker. With happy smiles, the mother and daughter leaned back in their chairs, sipping their wine and swapping old stories.

As the evening relaxed, John smiled and admitted to Mia, "I still have to admit I'd love that little flute for my collection. It would be the crown jewel of the whole lot."

Richard made an inarticulate sound.

"Now, Richard," John reassured the curator,

"I'm just saying I wish I could buy it for my collection. The local museum is the next best thing to owning it myself, since the Spinels think it should be in a public collection. I'm spending a lot of money on that museum wing so it's housed properly. I'm just not sure it's going to be properly appreciated there."

"A public collection is the only possible place for a discovery of this importance," Richard told him pedantically, made bolder by the wine.

"So you say." John was clearly not convinced. "I've never been a fan of showing our most important finds to the unappreciative masses."

"That's, that's absurd," Richard was almost speechless at John's opinion. "Important finds like this can't possibly be left in private hands. Think of the research that needs to be done." His round brown cheeks deflated, leaving his mouth open in shock.

"I know of a few important finds that mysteriously went missing or were simply sold off from museums after the donation fanfare wore down. Museums are businesses, like anything else. Don't pretend they don't sell off assets to the highest bidders when their balance sheet looks bad," John said, putting his glass down with a thump. "Very few museums even show most of their collection to the public. They just hide donations away from everyone and say it's for research. Who knows what salable artifacts are actually stored in the basement vaults that no one is allowed in?" he added with a sly grin. "Quite a few inventories have come up short of what museum donors thought were there."

Richard was definitely incoherent now. "My museum would never, never..."

John guffawed. "Just pulling your chain, Richard. You should see the look on your face." He took a long drink of bourbon. "I'm sure you'll take care of it." His smile became wickedly wide, like a wolf sighting prey. "And if you don't want the flute anymore, you know where you'll find your highest bidder."

Richard's glasses were sliding down his nose, and his pudgy fingers balled up the tablecloth. He clearly didn't know what to say to one of his biggest museum donors insulting museums.

Mia cut in, "I'm sure the flute will be in good hands with you, Richard." She smiled sweetly at him, "And I know our donor contract won't allow the museum to sell it." She turned to John, "So don't worry, it's safe."

"For now," John growled under his breath.

Mia continued, "And you'll realize how many people appreciate the bone flute when you see the crowds coming next weekend."

Estela tapped her husband's hand and said lightly, "I know everyone will love to see it. Such a wonderful exhibit. And it will raise enough money so the museum will show it beautifully to everyone, as it should be."

"They'd better," John said sourly. He pushed back his chair. "Well, honey, I'm ready to turn in. Thanks for dinner, Mia."

"It was a delicious dinner," Estela said appreciatively. "We will see you soon, Mia."

"I'm sure we will all meet in the next few days." Mia stood up. "I'm going to turn in as well." She smiled at Richard and Susan. "It has been a busy few days."

As she passed Sam, he played the first few bars of a lullaby, smoothly transitioning to a Bach sonata. He was still completely alert at the late hour, straight brown hair standing in all directions. His clever fingers moved in their complex dance over his guitar with complete ease.

Mia captured Susan's arm purposefully, steering her toward the restaurant doors. The poor girl was on the verge of a panic attack, and the exhibit hadn't even started yet. When they were out of the restaurant, Mia quietly told her, "Susan, dear, you need to get some rest tonight. The exhibit will go well, I'm sure of it. You need to stop work and get a good night's sleep so you're fresh for tomorrow. Go home and sleep. There's nothing more you can do tonight."

Susan pushed the sparkly clip back in her hair, creating snarls. "I was just going to take care of one or two little things..."

"No," Mia ordered her. "You are going to get a good night's rest. No more work tonight." With a slight frown, she looked the young woman up and down appraisingly. "Tomorrow, wear all black."

"All black? Why?" Susan asked curiously.

"Black is a good neutral color for business," Mia told her. "It doesn't distract people. You need to wear all black when you're working. You'll look much more professional, like wearing a uniform without that formality." It was also very difficult to have all black not match.

Susan looked slightly mulish, but clearly didn't have enough of a backbone to argue. "Okay," she agreed with a poorly hidden yawn.

"Go get some sleep now, dear," Mia told her kindly. Susan had the potential to be an excellent event planner with time and a little guidance, Mia thought as she watched her slumped figure retreat. What Susan really needed was a mentor to teach her how to be an event organizer for a hotel. She wasn't ready to be running the show, even though she was the one in charge. That made for an awkward situation, since it wasn't Susan's fault she'd been promoted before she was quite ready, so she was learning on the job. Mia's impression was that Mr. Lagarto would have hired the first person who applied, so he wouldn't have to conduct more tiresome interviews.

Mia looked around the cavernous lobby. Without guests filling the room, every sound echoed off the high wooden ceiling and unglazed terracotta Saltillo tiled floors. Only the night concierge, James, remained, nodding at her in greeting before turning back to whatever he was doing on his computer. She delicately hid a yawn, heading toward her cottage and her bed.

To Mia's surprise, as she approached the doors, Richard waited to intercept her, his stubby legs dangling on the deep leather sofa. Struggling out of the sofa with a grimace, he hailed her, "Mia, I'm so glad I've caught you."

She paused and looked at him, trying not to

show her irritation. "Yes, Richard? Can it wait until morning?"

"It will just take a minute. I just wanted to make sure you knew about something rather important." He pushed his glasses up owlishly and ushered her to a chair. His brown eyes looked directly into hers, imploring her to listen.

Mia perched on the edge of her chair, hoping this wasn't another of Richard's one more little things that would end up taking all night.

He pushed his glasses up again and said, "Look, I know I was a bit of a jerk to Kyle tonight, but that fraud doesn't have any business talking about archeology."

"Richard, I know that you don't like Kyle. We're not relying on his academic credibility, but his popularity. We want as many people as possible coming to the exhibit," Mia told him with asperity.

"That's what I'm saying," he told her, puffing out his cheeks for emphasis. "Kyle was caught a few years back with a fossil he'd smuggled. Absolutely perfect example of an Australopithecus africanus, over three million years old." His slightly smug gaze was steady on hers.

"Kyle was caught?" Mia hadn't heard anything about this. She wasn't sure she believed it either, with the sniping the two men had done tonight.

"Yes. The production company hushed it up, but my museum was involved since we'd sponsored the dig, so I heard about it at the time." He reassured her, "The important finds would have stayed in the country, of course." His eyes briefly slid away, then returned. "Kyle stole the fossil from the cave site while he was filming it."

"Why wasn't he prosecuted?" This certainly had not come up with anyone Mia had asked about Kyle. Difficult to work with, yes, that had come up, but absolutely nothing about thefts.

Richard's eyes slid sideways. "Well, it was actually found inside a camera bag, so he claimed it was his cameraman. And his cameraman claimed he knew nothing about it."

"So there's no proof Kyle was actually the thief?" Mia asked with decision.

Richard shrugged. "He was up to his ears in gambling debt at the time, most of which had been miraculously paid off in record time. I mean, he had tough-looking men showing up at the digs he filmed, looking for him. Several smaller finds had gone missing during his documentaries, and word had spread. After he was caught in South Africa, all the mysterious disappearances of small, valuable objects at his documentaries stopped abruptly." He shrugged, admitting, "Nothing has ever been conclusively proven against him, but I heard through the grapevine, Kyle's back in debt to some not-so-nice guys again."

Mia said impartially, "He has written some bestsellers. That can make quite a lot of money."

"Not enough for that kind of gambling," Richard snorted inelegantly, soft curving belly jiggling with laughter and brown cheeks curving in a sardonic grin. "No, my guess is that Kyle only got caught stealing once, but it had happened a lot more than that. He's still working with the same cameraman, too. I can't think why the man stays with Kyle, but he does. Maybe he's in on it too."

"Why are you telling me all this?" Mia lifted a delicate eyebrow.

Richard looked at her, disbelief showing through his slipping glasses. "Kyle's going to have full access to the bone flute tomorrow. And tonight you told him there's no security on it until after his show films."

2

A Fine Production

After Richard's story last night, Mia had made a quick detour by the exhibit hall. She'd mentally thanked Mark on seeing the professional-looking guards installed outside the exhibit room. Finally making it to her casita, she'd gone peacefully to sleep.

A sunrise glow across the desert woke her. Distant mountains glowed warm and bright as she sipped fresh orange juice at breakfast outside on her terrace. She savored the perfect moment, the bright acid sweetness of the orange juice, the golden sun slowly unfolding over the mountains. Small birds chirped morning greetings from outside her patio.

Small perfect moments, strung together like precious jewels, made life wonderful, she thought. Joy is never about the huge things, but the little moments in an ordinary day. The trick was finding those moments and cherishing them.

She sighed in complete contentment.

Reluctant to leave the sublime view, she rose anyway—she had work to do. Mia reluctantly rose and stretched, ready to begin her day.

Looking in the mirror, she arranged her airy pale pink blouse so that it just skimmed over white pants. A narrow, dark pink belt defined her waist, and pink spinels adorned her ears. She placed a substantial ring on her left ring finger, remembering her husband, Leo, giving it to her, with a soft smile. Even several years after his death, Mia still missed him every day. She certainly could have used his help today. Carefully smoothing soft pink lipstick over her mouth, she planned her day.

She wondered if Kyle Lee would try to steal the flute while he was filming the documentary finale today, since he wouldn't have access after that. Normal Spinel Hotels' event security was completely up to the challenge, but nothing was normal about the current hotel's security, still very much in transition. Their security risk was far from just the flute. There were artifacts borrowed from the museum and some of the museum's most prominent patrons, like the Wallaces. The silent auction donations totaled enough to more than pay for the museum's new wing. Mia didn't think the hotel's insurance company would be at all pleased with the lackadaisical security arrangements, even with the extra guards.

Well, there wasn't anything she could do about the problem, except keep a close eye on the filming today, with special attention to Kyle Lee and his cameraman. She gave the mirror a final approving nod and went briskly out to face her day.

The young concierge, Atsa, was on duty at the front desk this morning. Atsa was by far the most efficient person Mia had found at the Desert Sunrise Resort, and she only worked part-time. She was surprised when, for the first time Mia had seen, Atsa's wide red mouth wasn't curved in a cheerful smile.

Her cheeks drooping, Atsa carefully said, "Ms. Mia, you're not going to like what they've done to the exhibit."

"What do you mean?"

"That film crew—they've moved everything in the ballroom. Absolutely everything. I don't see how we can possibly be ready for the event in time." Atsa's black eyes dimmed further, looking worried. "Can I speak with you privately sometime today? There's something I think you should know about." At Mia's nod, she turned with a smile to a hotel guest coming up to the desk.

After Atsa's warning, Mia warily entered the exhibit hall.

Atsa had not exaggerated. All the carefully placed exhibits had been moved, from across the room to ever so slightly out of place. Deep drag marks on the parquet floor followed each display case, leaving gouges in the polished finish. Half the neat labels that had carefully accompanied each item were strewn across the floor, dirty and wrinkled. Cables snaked everywhere, ready to trip anyone, and lights glared white hot.

Mia stood still for just a minute, aghast at the cleanup now needed to have the exhibit ready for the preview party tomorrow night. This was not at all what she'd discussed with the director. After a minute, she gave a mental shrug. If it had to be done, it had to be done. That was a problem for later today, she thought, narrowing her eyes at the ruined floors. This was definitely the last time this film crew would be invited to one of her hotels.

A harried woman rushed up, barring Mia's way with a flapping hand, clutching a sheaf of disorganized papers. Her slim arm strained to hold them. Mia recognized one of the restaurant guests from last night, the woman who had been so obviously late joining her dinner companion. "Excuse me, I'm sorry. This area is closed to the public. You'll have to leave right now. We can't have any outside people here. I'm sorry." Her straw-brown hair looked like a haystack, clumped and scattered, as if she had forgotten to brush it.

Mia looked around the hectic room for help, and Kyle Lee strode suavely up, perfect smile gleaming only for Mia, "Mia, darling, so glad you could come." He explained to the woman ineffectually barring her way, "Mia is the hotel owner, Emily, dear. She's a very important indeed VIP. She can go wherever she wants." Taking Mia's elbow, he ushered her further into the room. He looked down at Mia, very conscious of the charm oozing from his smile. "Emily does all the boring things around here, schedules, research, equipment repairs, and all the rest of it. She keeps the rest of us on our toes," he condescendingly explained.

Emily made a face at Kyle that was half ingratiating smile, half grimace, and scuttled off with her papers, already beginning their inevitable fall to the floor below. Kyle smirked, "Emily always gets a bit unsettled on production days. She just can't learn to relax."

Gesturing grandly at the chaos, Kyle proclaimed, "And this is behind the scenes at a movie production." He took a long drink from a monogrammed thermos bottle. The smell of coffee and Irish whiskey wafted toward her.

A bit early to be drinking on a work day, Mia thought, but politely said, "Thank you for asking me, Kyle. I'm sure it will be an interesting experience." She noted several uniformed security guards monitoring the room with professional eyes.

Kyle took hold of her elbow again, steering her through the room. "Everyone, this is Mia, the hotel owner who's been lovely enough to ask us to film her find. Isn't she just wonderful?"

Someone important looking in a tall folding chair called out, "I thought the flute belonged to the museum?"

Mia started to answer, but Kyle slipped in smoothly, "No, it's all Mia's until she donates it. That's why that tubby museum curator is being so nice to you, isn't it, Mia, darling? She might decide to sell it for some real money instead. Not that she needs it." He squeezed her elbow conspiratorially, and Mia gently removed his hand, giving a little cough to deflect him. "Richard really wants to get his hands on that flute." He laughed disparagingly. "It's too bad he's never gone out in the field for real finds of his own, as I have." His studied smile showed just the right amount of boyish charm.

"Thank you all so much for letting me see behind the scenes," Mia said to the room at large. "Now, Kyle, show me where I won't be in the way, but still see everything."

Kyle imperiously ordered Emily back, still toting her paper stack. She looked annoyed at his peremptory treatment. "Emily, find somewhere for this lovely lady to perch." He told Mia, "I would get you settled myself, but I need to get my makeup done for the cameras." He smiled, letting her have the full force of his fascinating smile one more time. He walked to the service door, like a king striding to his throne. Mia noticed several female eyes avidly following him.

The woman nodded at Mia, blurting out in a rush, "Hi, I'm Emily Peters, the production assistant." She resettled the sheaf of papers, making them even more precarious.

"You seem busy, Emily," Mia commented. "Is it always this hectic while filming?"

"You would not believe," Emily began in a rush, shoulders curved protectively around the sheaf. Her deep-set brown eyes slanted downwards, like a sad hound dog, huge in her thin face. "I've been on dozens of shoots with Kyle. They're all like this to start." She smiled insincerely, tucking unkempt brown hair behind her ear, "But it all comes together in the end." Her expression seemed to say otherwise, but Mia chose to ignore that.

"That's good," Mia said. "I suppose you've had

the opportunity to travel all sorts of exciting places, too."

"Well, yes," Emily mumbled, looking at the floor and scuffing her toe on a scrape in the parquet. "I mean, this one is just Arizona, I mean, I used to come here when I was a kid. But we've been all over the world, Iceland, South Africa, Gibraltar. Anywhere Kyle decides is an interesting enough find to film. I plan all the travel and filming arrangements." Her face wilted a little at the thought of all that planning.

"South Africa?" Mia asked with a cheerful smile. "I've never been there. Is it as beautiful as it looks in pictures?" She'd always planned to visit the country, but only seemed to go where there were Spinel hotels involved.

The sheaf of papers Emily clutched finally gave in to gravity, scattering everywhere. She quickly knelt and started gathering them up, her thin hands shaking with embarrassment. "I'm sorry," she apologized. "Just a sec, I'll find a place for you."

An assistant raked a cable over the stack, scattering it further. With a frustrated mew, Emily frantically continued stacking papers up, huddling over them protectively.

Mia took the opportunity to find her best vantage point. Over on the far side of the room, a tired-looking man hunched beneath a big camera. She angled to a seat behind him. "Hello, I'm Mia Spinel," she introduced herself.

"Yeah, I heard Kyle. You're the one who set this up," he told her. "I'm Pete, Kyle's cameraman."

"So I guessed." Mia settled herself into one of the chairs lined up against the wall. "Have you been with Kyle long?"

"Seems like forever," Pete chomped gum angrily. "Yeah, me and Kyle go way back to when he was doing the news."

"Kyle did the news?"

"Sure, you know, the Explorer Channel's news, not the evening news." He barked a laugh. "No, car wrecks and break-ins were never his gig. Kyle did a show on the latest finds in archeology, interesting science experiments, cute animals, you know the sort of thing."

"I see," Mia thought Pete must be the cameraman Richard had mentioned last night.

"Then he branched out to his own show. I went with him. Lots of us here did." He sighed heavily, "Worst mistake of my life. The show flopped, so here we all are doing documentaries again." He shifted his weight awkwardly, lowering the big camera in its brace to a nearby table. "Pays the bills anyway."

"That looks heavy," Mia said sympathetically.

"Weighs a ton," he agreed despondently. "My back is killing me." He massaged his lower back.

"You should get a massage at the hotel while you're here," Mia suggested.

Pete grunted, obviously not planning on it.

Mia continued, "So, do you like working with Kyle?"

"Pays the bills," he repeated. "Kyle's about the same as any talent. Always completely full of themselves." He gestured at the cluster of the production team huddled around the delicate flute. "They're all prima donnas, but whatever." He chomped down vindictively on his gum. "I'm trying to quit smoking, but doing a shoot always sends me back."

"It sounds stressful," Mia said sympathetically.

"You have no idea." Pete shook his head, stringy ponytail grazing his shoulders. "The stuff they do. I can't even count how many times we've filmed all day long, and the director says we're shooting the same thing again tomorrow, because some tiny thing was out of place. You have no idea," he drew the last words out with disgust.

"That's too bad."

"Sometimes, I think I'm just going to quit this business and shoot weddings." He barked a laugh. "That'd be a whole new set of prima donnas, though."

"Weddings can be very stressful," Mia had been in the hotel industry long enough to know that. "Still, they usually end up happy after pre-wedding jitters."

"Hah, that'd be a nice change," he chomped his gum. "Documentaries never end up happy. I've had to go and film something on the other side of the world six months later because it wasn't the perfect angle the last time we shot it. They're never done until it airs, and then you get the critics bitching. At least now we can just shoot tons of angles, not worry about film costs. Pre-digital days were brutal." He stretched and rubbed his back, then smoothed his thin ponytail. "And the cameras are lighter, though you wouldn't think so after you hold them up for a few hours."

A shrill whistle split the bustle of the room. "Hey, Pete," Kyle yelled, like he was calling a dog. "Come here!"

"His majesty summons," Pete hurried over to Kyle and the director's side. Mia watched them for a minute, all three forcefully gesturing in opposite directions at the lights. Clearly, they were in the wrong place, according to everyone, but no one seemed to have any idea what the right place would be.

Mia let her eyes wander around the room. Everyone appeared busy with their tasks, almost frenetically busy, considering they must do this job all the time. As she watched, two of the crew pulled more wires across the floor and set up a huge box light at a slightly different angle. They stepped back, discussing the lighting effects on a reflective glass case. One man tried to lift the case off the fragile pottery inside, but was foiled by the locks. He buffed his fingerprints off with a dirty shirt sleeve, scowling at the smeared reflection.

Light glare was not a problem on the flute, which had been uncovered for the filming. As Mia watched, one of the lighting guys put his hand out to move the flute for a better angle. As she cringed, Kyle grabbed the man's hand, clearly telling him off. The man, with a face like a pessimistic bulldog, returned to moving the lights infinitesimal degrees around the flute to find the best angles. Mia noticed an alert guard, bristling like a beagle pointing at his hunting prey, stationed next to the flute. His eyes were trained on the flute like they'd been tied there.

After watching the lights slowly shuffling back and forth for half an hour, Mia decided the guards could handle exhibit security, and she'd go find some more interesting places to explore.

Atsa was busy, gesticulating happily to the honeymoon couple, planning today's adventure for them. Mia smiled at them, holding hands, excited about Atsa's suggestions. Seeing people enjoy their experience was the best part of managing a hotel.

She headed for the stables. When Estela had mentioned the horses last night, she realized she hadn't seen the stable renovations, except on a blueprint and balance sheet. It was time to see them in person.

Outside the confined bustle of the filming, the air was still and calm. Not many people at the resort were up yet, and the air felt crisp and cool. She walked through the heady perfume of the citrus trees, saying hello to a few groundskeepers, already hard at work during the coolest part of the day. The grounds were beautiful, an oasis in the desert.

An immense saltwater pool beckoned, clear turquoise water with a wide beach zone. Deep red umbrellas ringed the pool, cheerful in the morning sun. A few people were already taking advantage of the warm water. One man swam laps doggedly, determined to swim his allotted length even on vacation. A few children splashed in the shallow end, watched over by parents having a leisurely breakfast.

And two men took turns showering under the rinsing faucet. Hiking boots had been tossed under a nearby lounge chair, and they had stripped down to khaki shorts, not bathing suits. She supposed she should be grateful they were wearing something, at least. Mia noticed they had apparently brought soap with them, since the ground beneath foamed with bubbles. The wiry man started singing off-key as he scrubbed his long hair, loosening it from its braid, while the younger man toweled off vigorously.

She frowned. Why were hotel guests showering here? The pool shower was designed for quick rinses, not daily ablutions. She made a mental note to tell the manager to put up a small sign, No Soap.

As she delicately avoided their sudsy runoff, the older man said, "It's such a shame they're locking these fossils up in museums where no one really experiences them again." He toweled off his long gray hair and pulled a tattered Grateful Dead shirt over his head. He had a thin, scraggy build, except for a hard, round paunch like an olive on a toothpick.

Tucking the foaming soap into a plastic box, the younger man carefully rinsed his hands and turned off the water with a harsh squeak. "They don't even let people touch them, trace their fingers along the ridges." He shook his head. "Most museums don't even let people see the artifacts, just lock them away in drawers where no one but some grad student will ever see them again. Imagine never experiencing holding a bowl held by a Pueblo Indian a thousand years ago. And that flute they found, no one will even know what it sounds like. Damn shame."

Obviously, the men were there for the exhibit. She wondered why they were showering at the hotel pool.

And now, she too wondered what the flute sounded like. She'd been awed by its fragile beauty. Now she wanted to hear its voice.

The stables were located far enough from the hotel that guests wouldn't be disturbed by, ahem, barn smells. Mia walked along the gravel road, looking up at the mountains. Deep purple shadows still draped the valleys, gradually lightening with the angle of the sun. The brightly lit peaks were bare, ochre rock, undulating through time.

The stables sat in the foothills of the mountains, convenient for a trail ride. The long adobe building was surrounded by green paddocks. A few horses grazed, still tucked into their nighttime blankets. She could tell the stables were doubling in size, at least, with the new construction mushrooming on one side.

An antique rust-coated truck with the word Police crookedly hand-painted on it was parked outside the stable. The old blue truck looked like it might not even make it to the end of the hotel driveway, not at all like an official police car. However, it did have Police written on the side, no matter how amateurishly. With that thought, Mia hurried in to see what was going on. A police car at a hotel was never good.

A tall, burly man in a worn cowboy hat with a sheriff's badge clipped to the brim tenderly cradled a horse hoof between his massive legs. As Mia came in, he lowered it gently to the floor and patted the dun horse's flank.

"Well, Miss Rebecca, I think she'll be all right.

She just needs a little downtime." Taking off his hat, he scratched his thinning hair. "It's hard to believe someone would ride her that hard after she'd thrown a shoe." He patted the horse again absentmindedly. "I think she's just a bit sore in the off leg. She'll be right as rain with a couple weeks' rest."

A tall, weatherbeaten woman said, "That's a relief, Hank. I couldn't believe it when I saw her limping in the far pasture this morning."

He shook his head. "Ought to be shot, a person like that." He noticed Mia looking at them and tipped his hat. "Ma'am."

Mia came a little closer. "Hello, I'm Mia Spinel, one of the hotel owners. What happened? Is she hurt?"

"She'll be all right. Person that'd do a thing like that should be prosecuted. And if I catch them, they will be." He tipped his hat back. "I'm Hank, county sheriff."

The tall woman said, "Nice to meet you, Ms. Spinel. I'm Becky, your stable manager." She patted the horse with a gentle sun-spotted hand. "This poor filly here..." She shook her head in disgust. "Someone's been stealing horses at night, bringing them back early in the morning. This is the first one that came back hurt, though. Rest were just plumb worn out." She tenderly led the horse into a loose box. "A week in here, you think, Hank?"

"Yep, that'll do her. Then out to pasture a few weeks. She'll let us know when she's ready to do more. I'll come and blacksmith again next week, just to make sure." He looked around the stable. "Now what can we do to protect the others from those varmints, Miss Rebecca?"

Becky ran her hand through her short-cropped hair. "That, I don't know." She gestured at a plastic sheet draping one exterior wall to close off the renovation dust. "We're pretty much open here. Anyone can go through a plastic sheet."

"What is the security here?" Mia asked.

"Basically none right now," Becky told her. "I asked Don for a guard, but he told me not to be an idiot, the horses would be fine."

Mia was horrified. "But they're not fine if people are breaking in and stealing them."

"Don said they were bringing them back, so it didn't matter." The tall woman's erect posture wilted just a little, like a sunflower in the noon heat.

"They ain't fine, that's for sure." The sheriff adjusted his hat again. "Well, Miss Rebecca, tell you what, I'll get some of my boys to do a drive by every night while the stable's open like this."

"Could they?" Becky looked hopefully at him.

"Well, sure, Miss Rebecca, anything for you. It's an ongoing crime, after all." He looked at the dun horse's head peeking out of her box. He smiled at her liquid brown eyes, feeding her some sweet feed from his huge hand. "Serious crime, hurting a poor dumb animal like that."

"I think I'll sleep here in one of the boxes tonight. I'll wake if they come again."

"Now Miss Rebecca, I can't let you do that."

"I'll have my shotgun, of course, Hank." She

looked impatiently at him. "And I'll call you if I hear anything."

"You're a damn fine shot, Miss Rebecca, but you don't know who's breaking in or how dangerous they are. We don't even know how many people there are." The burly man looked like he could take on anyone he cared to.

Mia broke in, "As the hotel owner, I can arrange for a security guard to spend the night until the stable is more secure. That is security's job. The stable manager should not have to guard the stables." She looked at the injured horse. "I really cannot believe Mr. Lagarto has not done that yet."

"I can," Hank grunted. "Man's useless."

"That's the conclusion I've come to, as well," Mia said tartly. "Now, I'm not certain about security tonight, because I've had to bring in extra guards for the exhibit, and I don't know who's available, but the new system there should be installed tonight. After tonight, I can assure you there will be a guard in this stable at night. We can't have people hurting our horses."

Becky gave her a quick, relieved nod.

Mia turned to Hank, "That's one thing I'd like to discuss with you, Hank. I actually came to the hotel this week because my son noticed someone online trying to sell the ancient flute we're exhibiting."

"That's new," Becky barked a laugh. "Trying to sell it before they stole it?"

"Exactly," Mia said. "So I came here to check on the exhibit security." She coughed a little, "The exhibit security was inadequate, to say the least."

"Online?" Hank said disbelievingly, "Most of the stuff online is just made up by people with nothing better to do with their time. I don't need no internet. I got books," he spoke in the measured tones of someone who knew wherein his trust lay, and he wasn't changing for nobody.

"But this is someone saying they are planning to steal the flute," Mia protested. "It's worth a lot of money."

"Ain't got no time for gonna steal. I'll take care of it if anything actually happens," Hank pronounced with finality. "Probably just some twelve-year-old bragging. Doubt he'll leave his mom's basement."

A little disappointed, Mia turned to Becky. "Well, Becky, I don't know about tonight, as I said. But I will be arranging for the stable security as soon as possible."

"Thanks, Ms. Spinel," Becky said, looking a little less exhausted. Mia guessed she'd been spending most nights at the stables, whatever she'd told Sheriff Hank.

"I'd like to go on a trail ride while I'm staying, as well as hear all about the new stable," Mia smiled. "And please call me Mia."

"Sure, no problem, um, Ms. Mia," Becky said, getting back to her comfort zone. "Just call me the day before, and I'll take you out myself for a private tour. It's really beautiful this time of year." She looked at her large plain gold watch. "Speaking of which, I'm due to take a group out in a few minutes, so if you all would excuse me." She nodded to the sheriff, "Thanks for coming, Hank. I really appreciate it."

"Any time, Miss Rebecca." He took off his hat to watch her stride off to ready the horses, a little wistfully. "She's a fine, sturdy woman, she is." He turned to Mia. "Well, Miss Mia, I'll be going. Glad that sweet little filly don't have anything lasting."

"I am too."

After the sheriff left, Mia looked around at the quiet stable, sunlight streaming in through the clear plastic. Most of the horses seemed to be out riding trails in the morning sun. She guessed riding hours started early in Arizona, before the noon heat hit.

The stable seemed well organized, considering it was a construction zone. Becky looked like an excellent stable manager. The horses were very well cared for, except for the worrying thefts, which were obviously not Becky's fault.

Mia wandered over to the big loose box. The horse was already asleep, snuffling a little in her dreams. The poor thing must be exhausted, with such harsh treatment. Yes, she would have to go into why no security was in the stables, since this was not the first time a horse had been stolen.

The incompetence of Mr. Lagarto and the comparatively well-run hotel was a striking contrast. The new renovations were needed, of course, and would increase revenue and bring a broader clientele. However, the Spinels wouldn't have bought the hotel if it hadn't been a fairly profitable hotel already. They thought it would be a spectacular resort with some much-needed updating. She still could not understand why the hotel revenue had been reasonably solid under Mr. Lagarto's management.

Halfway back to the hotel, a man lay across the road like a speed bump, scraping a small sample of something into an envelope.

"What are you doing?" Mia asked with concern. "Are you all right?"

The man looked up, startled, then swung his legs around to fold and unfold into standing like some complicated origami crane. "Hi there," he peered down at her. "I'm fine. I was just taking a sample. Seeing if they'd been here yet."

"They?" Mia asked, then recognized the eager face of the UFO reader she'd noticed at dinner. Still, she had to ask. "To whom are you referring?"

"The visitors," he pointed a bony hand at the sky. "I was going to wait to visit until the observatory was finished, but there were strange flashes in the night sky two days ago. So I came."

"Strange flashes?"

"UFOs for sure." He gleefully rubbed his hands together. "What else could it be?"

"I don't know," Mia said carefully.

"So I'm checking for trace amounts of radiation, zinc, and phosphate." He held up the little glassine envelope. "I have a travel lab back at my hotel room."

"Interesting," Mia just had to explore this further. "So you can tell if UFOs have landed by chemical traces?"

"Absolutely," he assured her fervently. "I don't think they have yet, though. They usually do a few reconnaissance flights, then in the next few weeks, they land. I had heard one other report of night flashes, but the ones the other night were much bigger."

"I see." Mia thought of telling him of the strange horse thefts and returns, but decided that would probably encourage him too much.

"So I had to come here immediately." His eager smile beamed. "I hope I'll finally get to see a real live alien!"

"Very exciting news," Mia told him. "I'm Mia Spinel, by the way. One of the hotel owners."

"Are you? That's fantastic. I'll keep you up to date on everything that happens, don't worry."

His elbows flapped as he shook her hand. "I'm Neal Mjesec, chairman of the Arizona Aliens."

"I see," Mia said. "Thank you. Please do keep me up to date."

"With pleasure." He popped open a lurid energy drink and hospitably asked, "Want one?"

"No, thank you." Mia repressed a shudder.

He guzzled the drink down, Adam's apple bobbing visibly. Then, stowing the empty can neatly in a bag, he folded it into a complicated shape, elbows and knees out at right angles. "I'm just going to do a few more samples. Can't do just one, you know. Not scientific."

3

Hotel Gossip

Atsa was still busy when Mia returned to the hotel. Mia caught the young woman's eye and motioned up to the balcony level. Atsa nodded slightly and continued talking with the couple in front of her, enthusing over trail ride adventures. The two boys Mia had noticed at dinner the night before stood behind their parents, shoving each other when their parents weren't watching. Mia smiled a little, remembering the extreme effort involved in keeping young boys calm in hotels. She hoped Atsa would recommend sufficiently energetic activities to exhaust the boys—at least for a little while.

The sweeping front stairs, made of beautiful, polished wood worn down by generations, led to a long room with a view of the mountains, dramatically framed by long glass doors. Mia paused on the empty terrace outside for a minute, taking in the sublime landscape.

Mountains dominated the view, but most of the low hotel buildings spread out like an elaborate quilt beneath her, connected by the weaving green balls of the citrus grove. The large pool was busy now, sunbathers relaxing in the shallows and people splashing a large ball around at the deeper end. The stables were faintly visible in the foothills, construction workers moving purposefully around the half-built addition. She peered up into the mountains in the direction of the new observatory, but couldn't see any signs of that construction site.

The hotel undulated in low folds, molding to the land around it. It would be something to be proud of when it was honed to Spinel perfection.

She walked back down the long room, appreciating the dark hewn beams, framing small balconies onto the main lobby and other rooms. Her pink tennis shoes padded gently on large terracotta tiles. She thought the tiles would keep this hall cool, even in the hot Arizona summers.

She found the perfect high-backed chair, carved into intricate contortions, with an encompassing view of the busy lobby. Mia had barely sat down when a waiter appeared, saying imprudently, "Hi, Aunt Mia!" and bowing low, rebalancing the tray quickly as an icy drink shifted.

"Hello, Sam," she smiled up at the boy. Her nephew's tousled brown hair needed a trip to the barber, as always.

He collapsed into a chair opposite her. His

pants had shrunk in a recent growth spurt, so his socks shone in all their cartoon glory. Mia sighed inwardly and made a mental note to drag him shopping while she was staying. "So, how's it going?" He wiggled his shoes like they were too tight.

"Everything is just fine. Should you be sitting here while working?"

He waved a casual hand, "Nah, I'm filling in for a friend. I usually work in the restaurant, but it's my morning off."

"Yes, but," Mia stopped abruptly. His aunt telling Sam what to do was not helpful. His immediate boss calling him out for neglecting work would make much more of an impression. He looked at her like he knew what she was thinking and grinned winningly. She gave up resistance and smiled back. It was always a nice thing in life to know what was, and what wasn't, your problem. This one wasn't hers.

"I've had a lovely morning, visiting the stables."

"Yeah, they're going to be nice. Becky's let me lead some trail rides when they were short-staffed," he grinned. "Better than working inside, that's for sure."

"Until summer, anyhow," Mia told him. "She said someone had been riding the horses at night. One was slightly injured last night, but will recover with some rest," she assured him.

"Huh. That's not good," he looked off into the distance. "Who was hurt?"

"A lovely little dun," Mia told him.

"Socks. She's a sweet girl," Sam said. "So what are you going to do?" he asked, knowing his Aunt Mia would have a plan.

"I'll get some security there as soon as I can, but that might be tough until this exhibit is buttoned up."

"Huh," Sam said thoughtfully. "Tell you what, Aunt Mia, what if I spend the night there? Just for a few nights until you can get real security and cameras," he assured her, pulling his gawky legs under him, ready for action.

"No, Sam," she told him. "It's a nice offer, but your mom would not approve at all."

"But the horses..." he protested.

"Sam, we don't know what the thief is doing at night. It could be one person stealing the horses or a gang. They might be armed." She shook her head at him, "No, that's not a good idea."

"Huh," he said, his eyes mulish.

A redirection was in order, Mia thought. "I ran into the oddest guest."

"That'd take some doing," Sam grunted. "Have you seen some of them? Right now, there's one woman calling to spirits every night. She sounds like she's yodeling."

"Really?" Mia was momentarily distracted. "Well, this one is a UFO hunter."

Sam laughed, "For real?"

"Absolutely. I found him scraping some samples up from the road, looking for whatever traces UFOs supposedly leave. He sounded quite scientific about it."

"Huh," Sam's monosyllable was a different

tone.

"He said there had been weird lights spotted around here."

"Really?" Sam held back a laugh.

"I suppose," Mia didn't say she wondered if those lights were connected with the horses. "Apparently, the lights mean more are on the way, so he came for the big event."

"Really," Sam's tone was pensive. "I'd like to see that."

"It would be something," Mia agreed. Someone a few chairs away waved an empty glass high like a signaling flag. "I think you're up, Sam," she nodded to the guest.

He sighed and got to his feet. "Duty calls, then."

"And I'd like an orange juice, please."

He bowed with a flourish, "Your wish is my command, milady," and strode over to take care of his guest.

Mia looked out across the lobby. From her high vantage point, she could see everything, from the reception table manned by Atsa to the main restaurant doors and the hallway to the exhibit ballroom.

A lone security guard in a black company uniform stood impassively at the entrance to the ballroom hallway, checking off the film crew. The production assistant, Emily, scurried by with a precariously balanced tray of coffees. The cameraman, Pete, strolled back carrying a heavy black bag. Susan Johnson, dressed in black and looking much more pulled together than usual, walked briskly down the hallway toward the exhibit hall. Mia wondered what Susan could be checking on today. All of Susan's and her work would come tonight and tomorrow morning. The poor girl was going to have a panic attack when she saw the mess.

Mesquite seemed busy, the headwaiter smoothly ushering guests inside. Mia looked at her delicate spinel-encrusted watch. No wonder, she thought, it was already noon.

She sipped her orange juice, realizing she was a little hungry after her morning walk. Every now and then, Atsa would glance up at Mia and shake her head a little in frustration. She certainly didn't show any sign of being able to leave, with the steady stream of guests coming through the main hotel for lunch and arranging afternoon plans. Mia wondered what the concierge wanted to tell her.

John and Estela Wallace apparently hadn't taken a picnic lunch riding today, after all. They politely waited for their turn at the restaurant entrance, carrying on what looked like a quiet argument. They certainly didn't look as relaxed as they had last night. Estela wore a bold orange swirling dress with a heavy gold torque necklace encircling her neck. Her hair was severely swept into a smooth chignon, and she wore strappy tangerine and hot pink Jimmy Choos, raising her height by several inches. She craned her neck from side to side, as if she were looking for someone. John seemed impatient, slapping his pants leg softly every few seconds and checking his Breitling watch. Tahoma finally ushered them inside, out of Mia's view. She wondered who they were meeting for lunch, or if they just wanted to avoid meeting Kyle.

The huge wooden entrance doors were thrown dramatically open, and the tall woman who'd dined with Emily last night strode through. Heavy hiking boots weighed down her feet, form-fitting leggings emphasized her long, skinny legs, and an athletic top glossed over an age-thickened stomach. Her high, frizzed ponytail and garments were wet with sweat and splattered with dirt, as if she'd been running through mud. Mia frowned as she noticed the woman trailed mud like slime from a snail across the shiny lobby floor.

Atsa motioned to a bellboy who ran to polish the floor, almost before the woman had disappeared through the hotel rooms' wing. She nodded silent approval at Atsa's efficient cleanup signal. The hotel was well run by the hospitality team, even if it didn't seem to be run at all by the slovenly manager.

From her desk, Atsa glanced up at Ms. Mia waiting on the balcony, her legs crossed with an elegant twist. The older woman sipped orange juice, seemingly content with people watching while waiting for Atsa to answer yet another question about spa hours and trail rides. A steady stream of people came to the concierge on their way to and from lunch, intent on planning the remainder of their vacation day. Atsa cheerfully smiled and answered questions, inwardly wondering if what she had to tell Ms. Mia was important enough to make the hotel owner late for lunch.

Finally, after scheduling a hot air balloon ride

for the following morning, she turned to her colleague, "It's all yours."

He nodded, "See you tomorrow," and turned to a guest coming up for help.

Atsa looked up at Ms. Mia, nodded once to herself, her decision made. She ran up the stairs with loping, graceful strides.

Sitting down next to Mia, Atsa beamed at her with her wide red mouth. "I'm so sorry I took so long to get up here. Thank you for waiting."

"Right before lunch is always a busy time at the desk," Mia told her. "That hasn't changed since I was a concierge."

"You were a concierge?" Atsa asked, curious. Ms. Mia seemed removed from everyday working life, always serenely elegant even after long days setting up the exhibit.

"Oh, yes," Mia looked down at the concierge desk, her blue eyes distant. "I worked for several years as a concierge. I gradually worked my way up to hotel manager. That job happened to be in a Spinel hotel," Mia smiled in fond remembrance. "That's how I met my husband, Leo Spinel. He'd make excuses to stay at the hotel I managed. One time, he was the only possible management choice to supervise a new guest cottage, new paint in the halls, a big event he absolutely needed to be there in person for—all sorts of ridiculous excuses. He managed to stay at least once a month, even when it was completely out of his way. It was the sweetest thing I'd ever seen." Her sapphire blue eyes softened, remembering his face lighting up as soon as he saw her.

"I didn't know that," Atsa was surprised.

"We had a lot of fun together," Mia said, eyes sparkling. "We'd go and set up a new hotel—or one that needed some work—and spend a few months until everything was perfect." She sighed a little, still grateful for the time they'd had together, then suddenly flashed a grin. "You never know what you'll see every day in a hotel."

"That's for sure," Atsa agreed fervently.

"That woman who covered the lobby with mud, you did very well getting that cleaned up quickly," Mia told her. "I can't believe she didn't come in a side entrance. Getting muddy on a hike is acceptable, but one does not come in through the lobby afterwards." Mia pursed her lips.

"Oh, Destiny would never stoop to a side entrance," Atsa said, laughing. "She's all about making a grand entrance through the lobby and bragging about her hike."

"Does she stay here often?"

"She does, complaining all the time; it's just not like the old days when everything was done right."

"She doesn't look that old." Most people who reminisced about the old days were elderly, in Mia's experience. "What kind of old days?"

"Oh, about a decade or so ago, a bunch of hippies ran the hotel. Apparently, Destiny pretty much lived here and loved every minute. Total scam artists, from what I've heard. Lots of spiritualist stuff faked up, psychics and Ouija boards, that kind of thing. All back to nature talk, but spraying toxic chemicals everywhere." Atsa grimaced, "It took until last year for the orange groves to get the organic label because of that. Absolute hypocrites." She shrugged in a quick, lithe movement and smoothed her braid. "They got caught in some scam to sell nonexistent gold mines or something, so the last company bought the hotel. They started with good intentions, put some money into renovations, then I think they ran out of funding. And now Spinel's bought it and is pouring money into making it exceptional." She grinned imprudently at Mia, "I hope this time it takes."

"How long have you worked here?"

"I started a few years ago as a maid, part-time. My great aunt's Chef Chooli Biakeddy. You know, the head chef at Mesquite, so she told them to hire me, I think." Atsa shrugged, "I can't cook for anything, but I can clean. Anyway, I still only work here part-time while I'm in college. It's good hours for a student."

"That's impressive. A concierge is usually a career track, not a part-time student."

Atsa blushed, round roses appearing on her cheeks. "Well, I filled in during an emergency, you know. And I guess I did okay, because Mr. Lagarto told me to work the desk instead of cleaning. It's pretty fun, matching people up with things they'd like to do."

"It looks like you're doing very well." Mia looked approvingly at the young woman. "What are you studying in college?"

"Astrophysics," Atsa blushed again and swung her long black braid around. "My mom was an astronaut, so I got interested in the stars."

"That's impressive, Atsa." Mia was not surprised at the difficult subject Atsa had chosen. She didn't seem like someone who would drift through college.

"My grandmother is a shaman, so that's why I'm good at knowing what people need. At the concierge desk, I mean." She was blushing harder than ever and looked down, fiddling with her braid, then quickly glanced up to see Mia's reaction.

"Interesting," Mia said thoughtfully. "So, shamans know what people want?"

Atsa grew a little more confident, "What people need," she corrected. "Anyway, I'm not a shaman; she just taught me how to read people a little to help them." She twisted her glossy braid, "I mean, telling them they'd enjoy a trail ride or a hot air balloon trip on vacation isn't exactly life changing."

"I see," Mia nodded acceptance at the young woman's unusual skill. "I'm not so sure you're right about it not being life-changing, though. Sometimes the right experience changes people's lives forever. I think people expect only dramatic events to be life-altering, but usually it's the small things, like seeing a beautiful sunset or going on a quiet walk in the mountains, that start a slow metamorphosis deep inside. Gradual changes to how a person sees the world are more lasting than sudden ones."

Atsa nodded uncertainly.

Mia continued briskly. "Are you looking forward to the new observatory? I do hope you were consulted, as a budding astrophysicist."

Atsa laughed, roses back in her cheeks, "Not me, but I did suggest my department head to the architect. I think it's going to be fantastic."

"I do too," Mia said warmly. "I like the idea of introducing the wonders of the universe to hotel guests."

"Making science a fun evening event, too," Atsa said slyly.

"Absolutely. Anything you make fun is something people want to do. People naturally want to explore their world. We just make it easy." That was one of Mia's favorite things to do, create unexpected fun adventures, things you couldn't find at many other hotels.

Atsa tugged at her braid and frowned a little. "Oh, I asked to speak with you because I wanted to tell you about something." Her luminous brown eyes creased in worry. "I told Mr. Lagarto. He didn't seem interested, but I thought someone needed to do something." She twisted her braid around hard, brown knuckles whitening.

"Yes?"

"I let Kyle Lee into the exhibit room a day or two ago. He's been staying at the hotel while they were filming the dig site and the museum, so he's always around." Atsa rolled her eyes expressively, "I mean, he is always hanging out at the front desk." She shrugged, "He told me he needed to check out the room before filming, which seemed pretty normal. Some of the production staff have key codes, but he wasn't on the list, so I had to let him in."

"Yes?" Mia wondered where this was going. From Richard's disclosure, she knew why Kyle Lee hadn't been given open entry to the valuable exhibit.

"Since a lot of the exhibits were already there, it was locked, so I had to unlock it for him. I stayed with him, of course." Atsa tugged hard on her braid. "Look, it may mean nothing at all, but when I entered the key code, I saw him filming me."

"Filming you?"

"Yes, he had his phone at his waist, turned to the keypad, not me." She shrugged a little. "He was filming me entering the key code. It couldn't have been anything else. Of course, I don't know why he was doing it. He might just not like the hassle of asking to get in the room." Atsa shrugged again. "I went to Mr. Lagarto, asked him if we should maybe change the key code, maybe up the security for the exhibit. He said no one would try to steal rocks, especially not a rich celebrity like Kyle Lee." Her concerned eyes met Mia's, "I thought I'd better tell you in case you wanted to know, since it's your hotel and all."

"Yes..." Mia's voice trailed off, and she surveyed the lobby, thinking hard. After a minute, she straightened up. "Atsa, what time do you get off work?"

Atsa looked at her watch. "About now," she said with a smile.

Mia saw the next concierge arriving at the front desk. "Then I'd like you to help me plan a little trap for Mr. Kyle Lee this evening."

"A trap?" Atsa grinned broadly. "That jerk grabs

my butt every time I walk by." She shrugged the crassness off as unimportant, "Part of the hotel gig, but only creeps do that. I'd be happy to plan a trap for him. Any time."

Mia was horrified—her hospitality team should never be mistreated. As a woman, she had recognized a potential creep in Kyle, but she wasn't okay with that behavior happening in her hotel.

She still wondered why Estela seemed so uncomfortable around Kyle. Had he made an aggressive pass at her? That would be enough to make John antagonistic and Estela uncomfortable. Whether he was a thief, like Richard thought, as well as a creep, remained to be seen. The sooner Kyle left the hotel, the better.

"Hmmm, we need one more person," As Mia spoke, she noticed Sam hovering with his tray and motioned him over. She told him softly, "Sam, Atsa saw Kyle Lee acting suspiciously around the exhibit. I'm a bit concerned about the security installation tonight. I'm not sure they'll finish filming in time, from what I saw."

"Really?" Sam looked expectantly at his aunt. "What are you going to do about it?" There was no doubt in his voice that his Aunt Mia would do something, and he wanted in on the fun.

"We," she emphasized, "are going to meet back in the lobby at nine o'clock tonight. We're catching him if he tries anything."

"I'm in!" he said gleefully, returning to his job with an expectant step.

"I'll see you at nine," Atsa smiled, her cheeks rounding, and her braid swung cheerfully as she strode away.

Cheerful umbrellas dotted the terrace overlooking the large swimming pool, providing shady seating outside for La Parilla. Choosing a table with a good view of the sparkling pool and lush gardens, Mia breathed in the smell of the citrus trees with pure bliss.

She was just perusing the menu with interest when she saw Pete, Kyle's cameraman, being ushered to the next table. His slumped figure looked ready to collapse. He'd clearly had a rough morning. "Hello, Pete! Why don't you join me for lunch?"

The cameraman smiled at her uncertainly, "Sure, Ms. Spinel, that sounds great." He fell into the opposite chair.

"Have you been staying here long? I know Kyle's been here a few days while filming the dig site."

"The whole crew stayed here while we filmed the dig site. I can't tell you how much I appreciated jumping in that pool at the end of a long, hot day in the desert." Pete looked around him appreciatively, "It's a nice hotel."

Mia nodded thanks. "We've been working hard on the renovations. I think they're finally coming together. How did the filming go today?"

"Terrible," he sighed heavily. "Everything that could go wrong, did go wrong."

"Oh, dear. You'll be filming this afternoon as well?" Mia had hoped to clean up the exhibit later today for the party tomorrow evening. That clearly wasn't going to happen if they were still filming.

"If we're lucky." The tired man let out a long, slow breath, smoothing back his straggly ponytail. "Lights were in the wrong direction or not even on. The other camera didn't have memory cards in it. Kyle's cues were scrambled in the computer. Then Kyle spilled his drink. Splashed everywhere. Fried a laptop, and the coffee stains needed a major cleanup. Even leaked inside a display case." He laughed shortly, "That's when we decided it was high time for a lunch break. Poor Emily had to take the whole thing apart to clean it."

"Oh dear, " Mia commiserated. She hoped no artifacts were damaged.

"Hal, the director, was livid. Turned bright red and screamed his head off at Kyle. He's going to have a heart attack someday if he doesn't calm down," Pete added with a resigned sigh. "I thought I'd finally get to practice my red cross training for a minute." He grimaced.

"These things happen. Some days are just unlucky."

"Kyle's going to be lucky if he finds another job after this. Hal is really mad this time. Kyle can't afford another screwup."

"I thought Kyle was enough of an expert he'd be the go-to guy for archeology programs."

"There's always a new kid coming up in the wings, ready to step in. Kyle's had some problems lately, and I've seen Hal headhunting hopefuls."

Handing Pete a menu, the waitress asked Mia, "Ready to order, ma'am?"

Glancing over the menu, Mia asked, "Just a minute, please, Susie. Everything looks so good, I'm having trouble narrowing it down."

Susie laughed and went to help someone else.

"It's such a lovely day for a poolside meal," Mia said. "I hate to be inside on a day like today."

"Yeah, nice to be outside after being cooped up all day." Pete smiled, looking at the menu briefly, then closing it with decision. He squinted his eyes at the turquoise blue pool. "I wish we'd wrapped up in time for a quick splash in the sun. Those kids sure look like they're having fun."

Two boys threw a colorful beach ball back and forth, shouting encouragement to each other.

"Ready to order?" Susie asked them with a perky smile. "I can tell you the specials if you want."

With a welcoming gesture from Mia, Pete ordered, "Roast beef sandwich and iced tea, thanks."

Mia said, "I'll have the grilled chicken salad with adobo dressing, please, Susie."

"Yes, ma'am," Susie bustled away, heels tapping staccato on the stone terrace.

Pete appreciatively watched her go, then turned back to Mia, "I have to admit, I won't be sorry to stop working with Kyle after this."

"Really? I thought you always worked with him."

"I've worked with him a while, that's for sure. Most of my career, such as it is." Pete leaned back in his chair, shading his eyes from the sun. "Kyle's gotten worse lately. I mean, he used to be just a demanding jerk, like all the talent. Now," he picked up his knife, tapping it on the white tablecloth, "he's gone off the rails."

"How?"

"Well, those iced teas he's always drinking are definitely the Long Island version. I've been in this business a long time, and he can put away more than anyone I've seen. He even showed up plastered to the dig site filming once this production. Hal said if there hadn't been too much work involved, he'd have canned him then and there. We'd have had to redo the entire production, though."

He looked up as Susie poured iced tea into his glass, condensation filming as the glass filled. "Thanks, honey." He took a long drink. "That hits the spot. It's always hot in a studio setup with all the lights. Better than desert sand getting in all the electronics though."

"It must be." Mia took a sip from her glass. "Will you be able to find work without Kyle after working with him so long?"

"Oh, for sure," Pete said. "I mean, I show up on time and sober. I do the job. That's a lot in our industry."

"In most industries, unfortunately." Mia had had far too many employees who didn't meet those basic criteria.

"Frankly, I've been angling for jobs without Kyle since he left me with a hot potato in South Africa. He put a national treasure, a human skull fossil, inside my camera bag. My camera bag! Thank God I could prove I wasn't anywhere near the bag after the skull disappeared — in the hospital getting X-rays for a sprained wrist. Never been so glad to pay a hospital bill in my life." He wiped mock sweat off his forehead. "I don't know what they do to people stealing national treasures in South Africa, and I do not ever want to find out. I check my kit real careful now when he's around."

"I didn't hear anything in the news about a theft Kyle was involved in?" Mia asked. She didn't say Richard had already told her the bare bones of the story. She wished someone had mentioned the thefts before she got Kyle Lee, the celebrity archaeologist, for the documentary at her hotel. Everyone she asked had raved about how charismatic he was and how he always drew crowds. Apparently, Kyle had some dark secrets that went along with his good ratings.

"Yeah, they hushed it up. The documentary was part of a national push for adventure travel there, so the country didn't want the bad press. They had their skull back. The film company didn't want to be liable for the theft, and there wasn't any proof who had put it in the camera bag, just that it couldn't have been me. Most of the crew had access to the bag when we were packing. Everything gets put in the shipping crates and checked off the list. A lot of people have access on the other end, too. It's not like it was my personal camera, just the one I use. Usually, no one would open the bag but me, but it actually belongs to the production company."

"I see. That makes more sense." Mia asked curiously, "Why did you think it was Kyle who stole the skull?"

"Kyle's the one with the gambling debts," Pete said simply. "Rest of us, we do the job, then go home to our families and real life when we wrap. Kyle gambles in his off time. And little valuable things, not national treasures, had gone missing from several projects Kyle worked on. He just tried for too big a score that time."

"I see."

"He's been drinking a lot more lately. I'm pretty sure he's in with the loan sharks again. Emily kept him in check when they were dating, but I think he got to be too much for her."

"Oh, dear." Mia was a little surprised that the conceited Kyle had once dated the mousy assistant. "It's such a shame."

"Yeah," Pete crammed the rest of his sandwich in his mouth. "Good sandwich. Your chef sure knows his job, I'll say." He took a long swig of his tea. "I'd better head back to the salt mines now." He looked around for the waitress to pay for his lunch.

"My treat," Mia told him, smiling.

With a surprised look, he said, "Thanks. I appreciate it." He pushed back his chair, then leaned forward, speaking softly. "Ms. Spinel, I'd make real sure that little flute was secure when the film crew is done. Your security seems lacking, if you don't mind me saying so." He paused, "My guess is we'll be filming through late tonight with all the trouble today. I'd keep an eye on it if I were you. It's got around that John Wallace is staying at the hotel, maybe trying to buy the flute away from the museum. Lots of talk about how much it's worth and how there's a buyer right here. Not many people around who would pass up a few hundred grand of easy money." He repeated confidentially, "I'd keep an eye on it."

"Thanks, Pete," Mia told him. "I intend to."

He stood up with a casual wave. "Later."

Mia slowly finished eating, savoring her salad. Several varieties of bold crisp greens were mixed with herbs, harmonizing well with the spicy adobe sauce and grilled chicken. Salads were one of those dishes that completely relied on the quality of ingredients, she thought. Limp lettuce or a syrupy dressing spoiled the entire dish. Fresh ingredients never disappointed.

She wondered if a poor choice of presenter would spoil the flute's documentary.

Mia looked up as she heard clumping steps approaching her table. Destiny, the woman who'd trailed mud through the lobby, shoved her boots, still muddy, under the table next to Mia. She looked at her watch impatiently.

Mia noticed with distaste that she still wore the mud-spattered leggings and exercise top she'd been hiking and sweating in. Turquoise beads wrapped her neck incongruously, clacking together repetitively as she shifted in her chair. Mia couldn't believe the woman hadn't showered and changed before lunch, with that much dirt on her outfit. Destiny glanced through the menu briefly, then called Susie back with a preemptory, "Waitress!"

Susie hurried up, radiating efficiency.

"You don't have any native foods on this menu? Any at all? It's disgusting, only serving these domesticated foods. Food here used to be wholesome native foods, not white man's garbage."

"Ma'am, our more local fare restaurant is Mesquite, inside the hotel. Outside, it's a more casual American dining experience," Susie pacified the customer.

Mia smiled. Susie was clearly up to her task.

"They wouldn't let me in the restaurant unless I changed, so I'm stuck out here today. For a restaurant located in a hotel at the nexus of Native American culture, you don't have a lot of native food options."

Susie offered, "We have a grilled vegetable platter that includes local squashes grown in the hotel gardens."

"Huh," Destiny grunted, long beads clacking together. "Is it vegetarian?"

"Oh, I didn't realize the Native Americans here were vegetarian," Susie commented. "Yes, the grilled vegetable platter is vegetarian."

"They weren't. I am," the woman informed her with intense pride. "I wouldn't touch animal meat if you paid me." Her voice rose in a screech, "Animal meat is murder."

Heads turned, and Mia saw a man bite into his delicious-looking hamburger with what looked like extra enthusiasm, juice running down his chin.

"I see," Susie said carefully. "Would you like the grilled vegetable platter?"

"And water to drink. You do still have spring water here? Or did you get rid of that, too?"

"It's spring water from the spring located on

the hotel grounds," Susie reassured her with a bit of a forced smile.

"I'll take that then," she barked. "At least you can't mess that up."

"Have you been coming to this hotel long?" Susie asked, clearly doing her duty to an awkward customer.

"Longer than you can imagine. I can't believe the awful way it's been torn apart. The Tibetan bells gone from the lobby. No gurus waiting in every room to guide people in meditation. No psychic readings offered whatsoever," Destiny accused with a glare personally directed at Susie. "At least the Spirit Guide Room is still here."

"I see."

"I wouldn't be here at all if you didn't have one of the strongest vortexes next to the hotel." She looked in disgust at the happy families splashing in the pool, the man eating his hamburger with blissful gusto, and the gold-trimmed greens of the orange groves.

"Vortex?"

"Girl, do you know nothing?" The woman laughed, a harsh sound like a donkey braying. "The Yavapai people painted petroglyphs all over the rocks, showing where the spiritual energy was the highest. I've been on mindful journeys all over this mountain range, searching for energy peaks. I've always known this place was special, a spiritual haven for the enlightened, but when they found the bone flute here, I knew I had to come meditate at the place it was found." Destiny closed her mouth with a snap and stared down Susie, eyes radiating arrogant pride.

"Oh, I didn't know that."

"You should have," the woman stated. "You can go now." She looked down at her phone in a clear dismissal.

Mia had an early dinner at an inside table at La Parilla that night, instead of another long feast at Mesquite, since she planned to catch a quick catnap before trying to catch a thief. She just knew there would be an attempt to steal the flute tonight before the extra security was installed.

She had stopped by the documentary filming this afternoon, hoping she could begin cleaning up and calling the security install team this evening. At that point, it was obvious there would be no final wrap-up until late, and they would be lucky to make that deadline.

Tempers were frayed, the director shouting all his orders. Kyle sulkily went through the motions, but barely mumbled his lines through gritted teeth while flashing venomous looks at the director. Emily ran around trying to do ten different things at once, a pinball ricocheting ineffectually through the room, leaving chaos in her wake. The outside security guard checked everyone in and out of the room, but Mia felt the flute was far from safe.

Mia didn't know why she was so sure a theft

attempt would be made tonight. Undoubtedly, Atsa's shaman grandmother could tell her what her subconscious had noticed, but Mia certainly didn't remember it.

Tonight was logically the ideal time for a theft. The most valuable artifacts had been stored at the museum until now, when they were on display for the documentary. Security was poor, and a few guards could be easily distracted. Mia had seen the hotel safe. The ballroom security was more modern. And a thief was already marketing the flute online.

None of those were really the reason she thought tonight would be the theft attempt. The air felt heavy, almost like a coming storm in the dry desert. There was a suppressed feeling of expectancy, a feeling that something was about to happen. She must have noticed something to put her on edge.

Mia thought back to all of her encounters over the last few days. Richard was unlikely to steal the flute here, at the hotel, when he could easily walk away with it at the museum. Of course, he might be the prime suspect there, unlike the hotel. He had told her about Kyle's gambling. How would he have known if he didn't gamble as well?

And Kyle Lee. Mia shook her head over her presenter. She wished she had had better contacts in the archeological field to ask before she had chosen the man. John and Estela Wallace would certainly have warned her about Kyle.

John really wanted that flute. His offers to her had gone beyond ridiculous, and Mark said John had made him even higher offers. If the Spinel family didn't feel so strongly that historical pieces belonged to the public, they would certainly have made a deal.

Would John have made a deal with a thief, even if he couldn't show the flute to anyone else? Mia didn't think he would care much if he couldn't display it, but she didn't know how unscrupulous John was. It might be enough for him to simply know he owned it, but he did enjoy showing that collection off at his fabulous parties. He was well known to be an aggressive businessman, but she had never heard of him actually breaking the law. He certainly loathed Kyle, though.

Atsa had brought Kyle to her attention. Mia was certain she had seen Kyle filming the key code, but why he wanted room access was a different matter. Some people just didn't like to be locked out of places. Mia had caught enough hotel guests craftily sneaking into off-limits areas to know people did some very strange things, often out of sheer nosiness.

The stories Richard and Pete told about missing items from documentaries pointed to one of the production team members being a thief. However, if she were a thief, she would certainly try to point suspicion at someone else, before and after committing a crime. Despite that, Mia still thought Kyle Lee was the person she expected to find attempting a break-in tonight.

Sam played the guitar softly by the fire, playing peaceful music to relax diners. She let the individually picked notes roll over her in a soothing stream. Sam was coming along with his music since she'd heard it last time, with screechy Christmas songs accompanying admittedly off-tune family caroling. He met her eye and winked comically, not pausing in his playing. Mia noticed with a smile that he had several pretty girls eyeing him with interest. He seemed slightly wary under her benevolent eye, leaving the stage a bit earlier than usual. She enjoyed a relaxed meal of grilled steak served with Pioppino mushrooms, onions, and peppers.

Leaving La Parilla, she took the long way back to her adobe cottage. Oppressive air vibrated with the coming storm. Clouds billowed on the horizon, blotting out the faraway stars. She hurried a little, shivering at the sudden temperature change as cool air blew through the distant clouds.

As Mia passed the Labyrinth, a circular meditation path laid out with stones, she saw Destiny slowly pacing around the spiral, head bowed in the dim light, her long, frizzed hair catching the light like a flame. Torches blazed around the circle, transforming the space into a primeval path marked with blood red stones. Suddenly, Destiny raised her arms, calling into the sky. The woman stood there a minute, silhouetted against the horizon, then her powerful arms dropped, and she continued following the firelit path.

Mia wondered what the woman's thoughts were, following that endless spiral in the night.

Despite the bright lighting of the paths, in her hurry, Mia still nearly ran into Neal Mjesec, crouched in the dark at the edge of a path. "Oh, Mr. Mjesec, I'm sorry, I almost didn't see you."

"That's okay, Ms. Mia. I'm just collecting a few

more samples." He unfolded into a standing position, long legs spread out for balance on the sandy ground. "I have good samples from the whole hotel grounds, just a few more places to go. Tomorrow, I've booked a trail ride so I can collect samples in the hills. After all, that's where the light flashes were seen." He grinned with eager anticipation. "I just know I'll get evidence of aliens this time. And maybe see their ship!"

Mia couldn't help picturing the tall man's legs dangling off one of the trail horses. Politely, she said, "I'm glad you're having a successful trip." She really didn't want him to get her beautiful new hotel entangled with alien hunters. While interesting to contemplate, it just didn't fit with the Spinel Hotels image.

"I am indeed." He stowed the glassine envelope tenderly in his satchel. "I expect to have very interesting results from these. I know if I sample enough places, I'll find evidence of a previous landing."

"I'm so glad," was the only thing she knew to say. "Well, good night, then." Mia thought his chances of finding alien traces in the imported flower bed soil were slim, but whatever made him happy.

"Good night," he called back cheerily.

She'd only made it a few steps down the path when she heard a startled yell behind her. Hurrying back, she saw a rising glow in the sky, floating silently in the shimmering puddle of light far above. A screech suddenly hissed out, echoing off the buildings, then dying down. The soft light drifted farther up, floating weightlessly, then an eerie humming sound broke the silence for a split second.

She heard Neal Mjesec breathing hard, not far away. He sounded like he was running a marathon. His harsh breathing was the only noise cutting through the still silence.

The glowing light bobbed in the air above them, completely silent. Then one more high-pitched burst of sound, a tinny crackle loud in the still night, followed by complete silence, only the fading glow moving slowly through the air before disappearing into the darkness.

"Wow," Neal breathed. "I can't believe we just saw that."

"I can't either," Mia said, a little grimly.

"An alien, wait, it was too small to be a ship. It must be some sort of reconnaissance drone."

"It was silent. It couldn't be a drone."

"An alien drone," Neal emphasized, rubbing his long fingers together in glee. "Wait until I tell AA about this." He saw Mia's careful look. "Arizona Aliens, remember?"

"I remember," Mia said. She coughed slightly, "If I were you, I'd wait before I told anyone anything."

"Why?"

"Well, you don't know enough about it yet. You don't want to swarm the area with idle sightseers who would destroy the scientific evidence," Mia said as she thought quickly. "Right now, it's just your word you saw an, um, alien drone."

"And yours," he broke in.

She said with precision, "I don't know what I

saw. I would certainly want to know more before I said anything publicly."

"Hmm," Neal's Adam's apple bobbed as he swallowed hard.

"We need scientific proof," Mia reassured him.

"I guess you're right, a lot of people could destroy all the evidence."

"And we need more evidence. I was so surprised, I didn't even take a picture. Did you?"

"Well, no," he said in obvious disgust. "I didn't even think of it. Stupid." He smacked his head with his hand.

"So if this is a," Mia paused, "reconnaissance drone, there should be more coming in the near future." Not if I have anything to do with it, she thought with fury.

Neal's face cleared into a beaming smile. "Of course there will," he said, with the happy expectation of presents under a Christmas tree. "You're absolutely right. I'll be completely quiet about this sighting, just do a full write-up, so I have an accurate timeline. More scientific. I'll make sure I have a video camera going for the next. Then we have proof." He rubbed his hands together in anticipation.

"Yes, but you'll need more than that," Mia said reasonably. "People see movie magic create flying objects all the time now. You need real, hard scientific proof." There, she thought, that will keep him busy and be nearly impossible to do, under the circumstances.

"You're right!" Neal's face beamed at her. His voice squeaked in excitement, "I'll need to keep this absolutely quiet so we can get real, hard data, incontrovertible evidence of the aliens landing."

"Absolutely," Mia encouraged.

"Still," he said, his eyes gazing wistfully at the dark night sky, clearly hoping for a return sighting, "It was an amazing experience, wasn't it?" He looked at her for confirmation.

"It was," she agreed with all the warmth she could manage. "Now, Neal, I'm going to head on to bed."

"Okay," he smiled suddenly at her, then returned to gazing at the stars, his thoughts light-years away. "I think I'll stay out here a little longer."

"Goodnight, then."

She heard an answering "Goodnight," as she walked back down the path.

4

Night Explorations

Late that evening, Mia waited for her two co-conspirators. She checked the hallway to the exhibit room before settling in the lobby. Two alert security guards in crisp uniforms nodded efficiently at her, noting her presence on a clipboard. She introduced herself to them and discussed the security, feeling somewhat reassured by their professional demeanor.

"Has the documentary crew all left?" she asked.

"Yes, ma'am, we're locked up tight for the night," Bob, the guard, told her. He was shorter than Mia, but had weightlifter muscles bulging out the shoulders of his gray uniform. "We finally checked them all out an hour ago and secured the room."

The other guard added, "They moved the bulk of their equipment out through the fire door."

"Didn't the alarm go off?" Mia asked.

"It's an old system. They turned it off at the

front desk. Just flipped a switch and it was off," he said, shaking his head. "I've never seen such a disorganized group. They kept returning for one last thing. One man, Pete, I think, kept going back for yet another bag he'd remembered. He must have gone in there ten more times after his so-called final checkout."

The second guard reassured her, "I escorted Pete in and out each time, ma'am."

"I'm sure you did," Mia told him.

He scanned his list, "Kyle Lee, you know, the archaeologist dude, stayed until the bitter end. He told everyone what to do, completely panicking over them possibly damaging the exhibits. He checked all the display covers himself and made sure they were secure. Wouldn't let anyone else do it. There are alarms on those, you know, ma'am," he told Mia. "Let's see... Hal, the director, was in and out. Nice guy, we've met him before on another job. Oh, and Emily, his assistant. I can't count how many times she was in and out of there."

"You'd think some of the men would help her carry the heavy lights and stuff," the other guard commented. "But they didn't. She hauled it all out to the van by herself. Some of it she could barely lift. Hal said they're staying here tonight so the crew can go to the party tomorrow, kind of a wrap party for them. I'm guessing there's something left behind still." The guard rolled his eyes.

Mia smiled. "Probably. I'll find anything left when I get the exhibit cleaned up tomorrow for the preview party."

"Preview party tomorrow night?" Bob laughed. "That's some cleanup job you'll have. Have you seen the mess they left?"

"I saw part of it," Mia said, a little grimly. She'd already lined up emergency floor repair for first thing tomorrow morning. "But we'll get it done and ready for the party on time. Kyle Lee is giving a talk at the party, so it's going to be busy," Mia told him.

She nodded to the guards. "With you both here, I know I don't have to worry about someone coming into the exhibit hall this way." With the two professional guards stationed at the main exhibit entrance, this door should be secure. The other doors were the weak points.

As she waited in the lobby, the night concierge, James, kept glancing at her, wondering what the hotel owner could be doing in the lobby in the middle of the night. Every time he risked a peek at her, she caught his curious brown eyes and serenely smiled. He'd smile back uncertainly and look down at his desk, pretending to be busy.

With the daytime bustle gone, silence echoed in the big room. Every sound seemed amplified, from James's pen scratching to faint sounds of the cleaning team working in the back hallways. Mia's eyes began to droop in the hollow emptiness.

Suddenly, a loud yodeling sound rang through the lobby, undulating louder and louder, building in volume and pitch to a high wobbling screech. Then it stopped abruptly. James looked up at the startling sound, then down at his paperwork, shaking his head in disgust. Mia wondered if it could be some of the cleaning team's equipment? Maybe a minor repair to the building?

After a minute, the noise resounded. This was absurd. She went over to James' desk.

Looking up with a resigned face, he said, "I know. It's a horrible racket."

"What in the world is it?" Mia still couldn't identify the sound, sometimes harshly screeching, like raucous parrots, sometimes unpleasantly deep, like echoes from a black hole.

"It's the spirit room," he stated, his voice flat. "The Spirit Guides Room."

"The spirit room?" Mia said with an incredulous stare. "You mean ghosts make that racket?"

He laughed a little, "Not ghosts, though it sure sounds like it." The screech was rising to an unbearable pitch before it blissfully ceased.

"So what is that, that terrible noise?"

"We've checked, don't worry. This is the only place you can hear it." He saw Mia's face. "I know it's the lobby, but we try to keep the spirit room locked until late hours so no guests are disturbed."

"But what is it?" She was disturbed just knowing that sound was made in her hotel.

"It's the spirit room," he repeated. "Native American spirit guides and stuff, I guess."

"Spirits make that horrible noise?" Ghosts or not, their services would no longer be required, Mia thought grimly.

"No, just the guests are free to use it. Late at

night, like now." He sighed, his tired face sagging. "Look, it's been here forever. It's one of the old hotel features from when it was a, I dunno." He thought a second. "I guess a spiritualist center place. Lots of weird voodoo, like the spirit guides room. Mr. Lagarto said to just leave it during the renovation since some guests still use it."

"What exactly do people do in this spirit guides room?" Mia asked carefully.

James shrugged, "They call to the spirits, bang the gongs, play the native flutes, whatever they think spirits will hear, I guess. Apparently, people have to make a lot of noise to get the spirits' attention." He smiled, "All I know is we all hate this shift."

"I can see that," Mia said.

"I guess it's kind of like a meditation room," an ear-splitting shriek split the air. James winced. "Just louder. A lot louder."

"Who's making that horrible noise now?" Mia asked, her lips pursed.

"That tall lady with the beads." He pulled up a screen, "Destiny. She's staying in one of the cottages, the one next to you."

"Destiny? What's her last name?"

He turned the screen so she could see. "None given, just Destiny. Lives in California. She comes all the time and always uses the spirit room. Sometimes for hours." He pinched the bridge of his nose, like he felt a headache coming on.

"I see." Mia gritted her teeth as another yodeling call, competing with the sound of a big gong banging enthusiastically, rang through the lobby. "The spirit room will be closed permanently tomorrow."

James grinned at her, "I have no problem with that, but what about the guests?"

"Exactly how many guests do we currently have staying that use it?"

He shrugged, "Just Destiny right now. She's in there a lot."

"So as soon as she leaves tonight, lock the door and put a Closed for Renovations sign on it." Mia shook her head, "That noise. I have no problem with meditation. I like yoga. I think almost anything that soothes and enlightens your mind is worth trying. But that, that horrible noise," she searched for a polite word, "is not soothing."

The air vibrated with the gong reverberation, and a call like a tomcat on the prowl echoed through the lobby. James pulled a piece of paper out of his desk, writing, 'Closed for Renovation,' in nice, neat capitals. "As soon as she leaves?"

"Absolutely. If there are any spirits around, I'm sure they're hiding from that noise," Mia said fervently.

Her nephew and Atsa came into the lobby. Atsa commented with a grin, "The spirits at it again?"

James held up his sign. "Not after tonight, according to the boss."

"Thank goodness," Atsa declared. "Not many people come through the lobby at night, but the ones who do ask a lot of questions."

Sam grinned, "Unanswerable questions." He looked down the dim hallway and shook his head,

"Wow. That woman is batshit crazy."

Normally, Mia would have reproved Sam for disparaging a guest. She let this one slide.

"Why are you up tonight?" James asked curiously, now that the ice was broken.

Before Sam or Atsa could volunteer information, Mia answered quickly, "Atsa promised to show me the desert stars at night. It looks like a beautiful night, too."

The phone rang, and James answered it, saying into the instrument, "No problem at all. I'll be right there, sir." He hung up, placing a call for service button prominently on his desk. "Any brief breaks from that noise are no problem at all."

Mia laughed. "I don't blame you." She led her companions out the main entrance. "Come on, you two."

"Have fun!" James visibly cringed at a particularly high screech and rapidly walked toward the guest rooms.

As soon as they got outside, Sam said, with a note of panic in his voice, "Aunt Mia, I think I screwed up."

Mia just looked at him, her clear blue eyes steadily on his face. That look had always made her children admit all.

"The spaceship thing? It was me," he confessed, big eyes looking down at his feet.

"I know," she stated flatly.

"Spaceship?" Atsa asked curiously.

Mia informed her, "Sam played a trick on Mr.

Mjesec with a fake spaceship."

Atsa burst out, horrified, "You can't do that around here. People take that stuff seriously."

Sam glanced up to see Mia's reaction. "I didn't think he'd believe it, you know? I just thought it would be funny."

"Funny," Mia repeated. Her lips flattened with distaste.

"Yeah, funny, you know?" He tried to work his charming grin on her, but it turned sickly. "I just thought he'd think it was a good joke. Just fun, you know?" He wiped his hands on his jeans.

"Did Mr. Mjesec see it as a joke?" Her voice remained frigidly level.

"No, he thought it was real." Sam's voice was a mix of awe and disgust. "He really thought he'd seen aliens. For real."

Mia told him, "He was all set to call his group of alien hunters to scour the area for signs."

"Oh." Sam didn't meet her eyes. "He's going to call his group?"

"He was," Mia said. "They would have destroyed this hotel's reputation instantly."

"Yeah, a bunch of alien hunters running around wouldn't look so good at a family resort," Sam said hopelessly, shoulders slumped. Then he seized on a phrase, "Would have?"

"I talked him out of it. I convinced him he needed more evidence." She shook her head. "Luckily, he didn't have a camera recording. That would have made it impossible."

Sam's eyes lit up with his narrow escape. "Oh, man, my dad would have killed me."

"Forget your dad. I would have killed you," Mia told him, her voice tight. "This is our family business, and you are here, representing our family. Our family depends on the Spinel Hotels' reputation, and everyone in the family works very hard to make our hotels superb." She stared him down, and Sam's eyes dropped. "If I ever hear about anything at all, anything else like this, you are fired. Permanently."

"Fired?" Sam was aghast. He wiped sweaty palms on his jeans, his voice cracking slightly, "My dad would kill me."

"Yes, he would," Mia agreed wholeheartedly.

She started walking again around the hotel. "Now, be quiet." She motioned for Atsa to rejoin them from where she'd discreetly wandered off. "We're guarding the exhibit room from outside. One guard is stationed outside the fire exit, but with the landscaping and buildings obstructing his view, he can't possibly cover it comprehensively." She reassured her co-conspirators, "I arranged this beforehand with security, so they know who and where we are. The only way we can identify the thief is to quietly blend into the landscaping. We don't want anyone to notice us there."

Atsa whispered, "We're just going to wait outside the building? That's it?" She frowned a little, "But Kyle filmed me entering the key code at the main exhibit entrance. Don't we want to guard that door?"

"The simplest plans are usually the best. I checked the security in the main hall. Two security company guards, so I don't think a thief could enter that way, even if he knows the key code. There's simply no way to get past two hired guards. When Kyle filmed you, we didn't have extra security, so the main door was the easiest access. Hotel security alone would have been stretched thin, rotating between several doors. But the security company only had three guards available tonight, so they're relying on an outdated security system inside the room. It's a huge area for them to cover. The fire door is the weakest point now." Mia waved her hand at the long line of tall windows lining the exhibit room wing. Dark shapes of shrubs and trees were spaced out artistically, hiding the ugly bulk of the metal fire door. Any one of those shadowed clumps could hide several people without a guard noticing.

Mia sighed a little, "Not that any of the security is up to our standards. It would be very easy to sneak up behind a single guard in the middle of the night, so we're staying with him."

"What about the service door?" Atsa asked. "There's one in the back of the room to bring food in for events and things."

"We have two hotel security guards stationed there," Mia told her. "Anyone entering there has to go through the service entrance and card reader before they get to that door. I changed the exhibit room's passcode immediately after I heard your story." She nodded appreciatively at Atsa.

"So, unless it's an inside job, the service door is more secure than the main hotel doors, where there are several ways to get into the exhibit hallway. The hotel security team needs some," she cleared her throat meaningfully, "improvements, so I put the professional team on the vulnerable main doors you were quite rightly concerned about. From things I have heard, I think it is possible our documentary star, Kyle Lee, has pilfered antiquities in the past. Those doors are completely open to anyone with the key code. No security card required. And no guards on them until tonight."

Atsa made excuses, "Mr. Lagarto won't pay much for security. He says security is just there to bounce drunks from the bar anyhow. Once the guards have a little experience, of course they go where they make more money."

"I see," Mia said with icy precision. "There will be some changes coming to the hotel in the near future, but for tonight, our plan is to stand quietly and watch for trouble."

"Cool, Aunt Mia. Do we jump anyone who looks suspicious?" Sam bounced a little on the soles of his feet.

"Certainly not," Mia said, narrowing her eyes. "We try to identify them if possible, then draw their attention to the fact that they are being watched. They should leave, with four people observing them. Our object is to prevent theft, not run down thieves. That is the police's job." She sighed, "As gratifying as it might be to unmask a thief in the act, I would prefer adequate security and a good night's sleep."

"Do you really think someone's going to try to steal the flute tonight?" Sam's bouncing steps slowed with no prospect of exciting superhero feats in the night.

"I do. But a rather dull evening is what we hope for. There will be better security arrangements by tomorrow night. Your Uncle Mark is seeing to that." She waved at the side of the building. "We may be out here a long time. Find a comfortable position and stay in it. And be quiet." She looked hard at Sam, who was at the edge of a shadow, trying hard not to be noticed while scuffling his feet. "Completely quiet," she emphasized and pointed her two henchmen to well-spaced vantage points with plenty of cover. The guard scanned them closely on approach, nodding a silent acknowledgement of their presence.

Mia leaned against a large tree in the shrubs, after cautiously checking for snakes in the surrounding area. Her charcoal grey yoga clothes blended into the shadows. Not much light broke the darkness. At this hour, most guests were tucked up in cozy beds on the other side of the building.

She shivered slightly, drawing her sweater around her a little more. A dark scarf hid her bright blonde hair, so at least her ears were warm. Mia always forgot how quickly the desert lost heat at night. She rested lightly on the tree, trying not to move.

Atsa nestled in the deepest shadows of a tree, slowly letting her eyes adjust to the dim light from the nearby path lights and ambient hotel lights. Her mind stilled, and her senses went on high alert. The setup reminded her of hunting expeditions with her uncles, patiently waiting for their prey to arrive.

They would arrive at the site, hiking in pitch black night with only headlamps to light their path. They sat for hours, not moving. She'd quickly been cured of her urge to wiggle by her uncle explaining that if she moved and scared off the prey, she wouldn't be invited again. And she wouldn't get meat to eat. So she'd learned to be silent and still, waiting for dawn to unfold and the prey to appear.

Atsa hoped this would turn out to be a wild goose hunt with no geese in sight. With the professional guard there to actually capture a thief, she wasn't worried about personally getting hurt, but still, things could happen in a hurry on a hunt. Ms. Mia seemed like she could move relatively quickly for her age, but having the older lady in possible danger worried Atsa. Of course, she'd bet on her Aunt Chooli in any fight, and she was older than the mountains. Not that Atsa would ever tell Aunt Chooli that. She'd bean Atsa with her rolling pin if Atsa ever dared call her old.

And Sam, cute, charming Sam with his wide grin. Atsa considered Sam for a minute, deciding he was a nice kid, but not quite a man yet, despite his chronological age. He'd shown that with his UFO stunt. She rolled her eyes in the dark. Of all the stupid tricks to play.

Atsa didn't know yet how Sam would handle himself in a fight with a thief. Would he act like a boy or a man? All in all, it would be much better if this were just a boring evening where nothing happened. As long as it didn't storm, this wasn't too bad.

The night lay cold and silent. The rich smell of

orange blossoms floated through the air, wafting in on little breezes every so often. Occasionally, she'd hear the sound of some animal scurrying through the night. An owl hooted, long and moaning. Sam jumped in his hiding place, then muffled his sound quickly. The measured tread of the guard continued, up and down the building, only pausing at the far ends to survey the landscape. Hopefully, he would deter any thieves.

Atsa heard Ms. Mia's feet shuffle, just a little every so often, faintly scratching against the tree she leaned against. Sam shifted continually, sandy soil making faint squeaking sighs with every movement he made. His body was in constant muffled motion. Atsa hoped the thief wouldn't notice his fidgeting. If there was even a thief. She was regretting telling Ms. Mia about Kyle, but it had been the right thing to do. Her mom always told her to do the right thing, and what happened next was meant to be. Well, she'd done it, and here she was. Leaning against a cold tree in the dark.

Atsa focused on the dark rectangles of the long glass windows leading to the exhibit room and the dark silhouette of the guard walking. The air felt cold and heavy, faint stirring of a breeze in the dark night.

A leaf crackled like a sudden gunshot, directly in front of Atsa. A gray blur at the edge of the path started to come into focus. She heard Sam start at the noise, quickly stifling the crunch of his foot. The guard swung around and peered out. Another leaf crackled at a hasty retreat by the intruder. Atsa stepped out of the shadows to see who the person was, but she was too late. They had vanished.

Mia moved out of hiding at the sound as well, but quickly retreated to her tree, hoping she had been unseen. She was sure they'd startled the thief, since the person had left when they heard other people nearby. She wished Sam hadn't made noise, scaring the thief away before they could identify him, but it was too late now. Sam was a good kid and trying hard. It was difficult not to jump at middle of the night noises, even if you were expecting them.

Mia decided to stay at least another hour, just in case the thief came back. After all, there would be better security by tomorrow night, so this was the only time they needed to be here. Resigning herself to more quiet time with her tree, she let her body relax against the rough bark.

Her eyes were drooping a little, and she was thinking it was about time for them to call it a night when she heard a sudden scream, high and resounding through the night in pure terror.

Atsa's voice rang out, "The stables!" as she sprang out of the bushes. Mia saw her run like a young gazelle, lithely graceful. Sam closely followed Atsa, his athletic frame almost as fast. The guard, startled, looked at the others, clearly undecided on whether to leave his post or not.

Mia ordered the guard, "Stay here!"

Looking back at the fire door, she knew the ancient flute was now vulnerable with just one guard watching it. She gritted her teeth. With firm resolve, she ran toward the stables.

Atsa and Sam far outdistanced her, but Mia kept running as fast as she could, her legs given strength by the horses' terrified screams. She could see the flames far off in the distance, glowing tongues of orange against the dark mountains. The fire had not destroyed the stables yet, so Mia ran to help, spurred by the horses' terror.

What had taken her half an hour to walk this morning on her peaceful stroll took only ten minutes to run, even at her slow speed. When she got to the stables, Atsa and Sam were already leading panicked horses out of the stable as smoke billowed out the doors. Rapidly taking the horses to the furthest field, they raced back to save the others.

Becky, sickly green in the smoky air, was propped against the fence, blood running down her face from a cut on her head. She seemed dazed, barely able to sit up.

Mia ran to her, "Are you okay?"

Becky told her shortly, gritting her teeth in pain, "Fine. Jumped me from behind. Go get the horses." She stared at the burning stable, willing the horses to get out.

Mia didn't waste time arguing. She ran into the stable, grabbed a halter, and led the dun horse, Socks, out. Fortunately, Socks was sedate, still too tired and lame to bolt. From Mia's glance through the smoke, it looked like the fire had started in the new addition to the stable, so as long as they got the horses out quickly, they'd be fine.

The horse followed her obediently as Mia led

her into the far paddock. Going as fast as she could, Atsa still flew by her, racing for the others. The horses' frightened cries filled her head with no room left for anything else. The heat from the fire scorched the side of her face as she ran back inside.

Sam struggled with a huge white horse, terrified and screaming. He tried several times to fit it with a halter. The horse refused. It reared up, flailing with both feet against the loose box. Sam sprang out of the box, rolling to the ground and slamming the door.

He looked at her with horror. "I can't get a halter on him. What do I do?" The horse screamed in panic, and his hoof hit the box wall, shaking it violently.

"Open the door," Mia yelled. "He'll get himself out."

Sam did, and the horse cannonballed for the open stable doors, at a speed that would win the Derby.

"Don't worry about him now," Mia ordered Sam. "Get the ones we can easily halter in the paddock, and make sure the rest are out of the stable any way they'll go. Anything is better than that," she nodded at the flames licking the doorway.

Sam, face white, hesitantly opened another stall, halter still in hand. This horse was eager to be led to safety and the far field, running with him quickly, as neatly as in a show ring.

Mia picked another, thankfully, relatively cooperative horse and trotted it out. She wrapped her scarf around her nose and mouth and kept going, spurred by the screams.

Atsa flew past them again, loosened hair

streaming behind her in a flowing black wave. "The main stable has caught. Open all the doors so they can get out. We'll round them up afterwards."

More night crew came running. Security guards, the concierge, and several of the housekeeping team all opened doors as fast as they could, forcing the horses out into the stable yard.

They worked furiously, haltering and leading any horses who didn't run for safety on their own. The dark, smoky air was unbearable, but they kept going in for more. They coughed in the acrid smoke, trying to hold their breath while inside and drinking in great gulps of icy cold air outside.

When all the horses were out, they hurried to Becky, still lying propped up on the posts, eyes closed, her face pale as the post.

"Becky?"

Her eyes flew open, not quite focusing on them. To Mia's relief, she seemed fairly alert after what must have been a bad knock on the head, judging by the blood. Becky looked at the red flames crawling up the stable and asked in a hoarse, hopeless voice, "They out?" She tried to pull herself up on the fence post, her face white.

"Yes, don't worry," Mia told her quickly. "They're all out."

Becky subsided in relief. "Called the fire station and the police," she said hoarsely. "Here soon."

"Good," Mia sat down next to Becky. "And did you call an ambulance for yourself?"

"I don't need an ambulance for this little cut,"

Becky retorted. "I should check on the horses." She made another feeble attempt to stand up, clawing hands shaking with effort, then collapsed against the fence post again.

"Becky, relax," Atsa told her. "We'll take care of it. They're out of the fire, that's the main thing. And I've got hoses keeping the fire out of that paddock. It'll be a swamp towards the stable end, but no fire."

With surprise, Mia saw James and the guards playing streams of water, soaking the ground between the paddock and the flames. She hadn't even noticed Atsa arranging that.

Sam said, "I'll check on the ones here for you, but what about the horses we didn't get into the paddock?"

Becky shook her head with disgust, then winced at the movement. "Not much we can do in the dark." Supported by the fence post, she watched the flames clawing the night sky. "They're out of that, so anything's better."

The flames leaped as they ate into the main stable, growing hotter with the fuel. The air crackled. Intense heat radiated from the flames, scorching their faces. A water trough boiled like a bubbling cauldron, then its plastic melted into a puddle, finally consumed by the hungry fire.

Whinnying their fear, the horses huddled together against the far end of the paddock. A few more active horses paced back and forth, smooth trotting, then a quick jerk of their heads and a hard gallop when their opposite eye saw the flames. Their eyes, ringed with white and rounded in panic, renewed as they saw the flames anew for the first time. They snorted and shuffled, their mouths foaming white at the edges and nostrils flaring.

"Firetruck better get here damn soon," Becky said, shifting uncomfortably and squinting in the distance. "My guess is most of the loose horses will circle back here when the fire's out." She laughed shortly, running her hand through her short hair and wincing when she encountered the cut. "They know where the sweet feed is at."

"Should we try to look for them?" Mia asked.

"No, no point searching in the dark. If they make it to any of the ranches around, they'll bring the horses back home." Becky looked at the burning stable. Acrid smoke made her cough. Tears dripped slowly from her reddened eyes. She batted them away, annoyed at the weakness. "I don't know where we're going to house them now."

"Becky, we'll find a good place and get them there," Mia told her. "We'll get the stable done how you want it as soon as we possibly can. They'll be fine out here tonight." She gave Becky a grin, "After all, guests are going to want trail rides. We can't disappoint the guests with no mountain trail rides."

"True," Becky agreed with exhausted relief.

"The important part is you and the horses are all safely out of the stable," Mia said with finality. "Everything else is easy from there."

"Yeah." Becky still looked at the blaze. The fire was at full height now, showing through the roof tiles.

"Damn shame. It was a nice stable."

"The next one will be nicer," Mia promised. "Just think, you get to plan the next one from the ground up. I do insist, however, that there be fire suppression installed."

Becky barked a laugh at that, then closed her eyes in pain.

Mia sat there, looking at Becky's pale face, worried about her head injury. She stood up as she heard sirens. "The cavalry has arrived."

Atsa ran up, eager to help with whatever came next. Sam was a bit slower, easing himself gradually into a standing position and rubbing his shoulder, wincing.

Lights soon strobe-lit the ruined stable. The firemen quickly reduced it to a smoldering hissing ruin, a blackened structure with great pieces missing, like a half-finished jigsaw puzzle.

Sheriff Hank drove up in a hurry, lights flashing. He swung his legs out of the old blue truck and ran over to Becky, slowing to a respectable pace as soon as he saw she was okay. With a look of relief that said all, he nagged, "Now, Miz Rebecca, what did you think you were doing in the stable tonight? I seem to recall telling you not to sleep there—it was too dangerous." He bent down over her with concern.

"Now, Hank," Becky began. "I was perfectly fine." The blood still oozing from her forehead was not convincing.

"Miz Rebecca," he scolded, pushing his hat firmly on his head and sitting back on his heels. "You are not fine, and you're going to the hospital first thing to get checked out. Looks like you need a few stitches at least." He poked at the slowly seeping cut, and she swatted him away.

"Now, Hank," she remonstrated.

He interrupted her, "That's an order, Miz Rebecca. I've got an ambulance coming around to take you there right now."

"But the horses?" she protested weakly.

"They'll be fine," he reassured her. "I'll get things straightened up here and leave a few of my boys. They'll see to the horses." He straightened up, stretching his back tall. "Then I'll come along to the hospital and check on you. I'll bring you on home if the docs okay it."

"But the horses," Becky tried again, pain in her voice.

"No buts, Miz Rebecca. You're going straight to the hospital."

Mia interjected, "Sheriff Hank, there are still a few horses missing. A few bolted, and we didn't get them into the paddock."

He hooked his thumbs in his belt loops. "They're all out of that, though?" He looked with concern at the blackened stable ruins.

"They're all out, Hank," Becky said, exhausted. "But five ran off, wouldn't be haltered. Poor creatures just desperate to get away from the fire." She winced as she repositioned the cloth on her forehead.

His face cleared. "We'll find them for you, Miz Rebecca. Don't you worry about that right now. I got that." He awkwardly patted her shoulder. "Don't you worry. I'll put out the call right now." His eyes squinted at the far paddock, horse silhouettes lit up against the dark horizon. "Rest in there? Looks like that's most of them."

"Yes," Becky agreed. She closed her eyes, clearly struggling to stay awake.

"Looks like Lightning went running. He would," the sheriff said with a rueful smile. He looked down at Becky, worried eyes looking at her closed ones, lashes dark with moisture. His hand rested on her shoulder protectively. "That dang horse is nothing but trouble."

Becky didn't answer, her eyes closed.

"He did, sir," Sam spoke up. "I couldn't hold him, so I let him out." He looked down at grubby, torn hands. "I'm so sorry."

"They're out of the stable. They're alive. We'll find them," the sheriff reassured Sam, but his words were for Becky. "Where's that dang ambulance?" he asked, looking out over the desert.

Atsa told him, "The ambulance takes thirty-five minutes to get here. The fire station is only ten minutes away."

They looked at her.

She shrugged, "I'm the concierge. Guests want to know that stuff when they're hurt."

Mia calculated, looking at her watch. "Then it should be here any minute." She looked at Becky's face, still and white as a marble statue. "I think she's just exhausted, Sheriff. It sounds like she's been trying to stay up, looking for the horse thieves, and they hit her from behind."

He nodded. "She'll be right with some stitches and a good night's sleep." He pointed at the incoming ambulance lights. "And I'll find her horses for her. That's what she really needs."

The ambulance EMTs went to work quickly, carefully escorting the weakly protesting Becky up the stairs and wrapping her like a mummy in a blanket. Her worried eyes searched for Hank, relaxing when she saw him at her side.

"I'll be along once I clear this up here, Miz Rebecca," he reassured her, and she nodded, closing her eyes. "So long, then." He closed the doors, and the ambulance was off, lights and sirens calling. He looked after it with a frown.

Mia broke him out of his concentration. "What can I do to help, Sheriff?"

A little startled, he looked down at her, tipping his hat back. "Not much, Miz Mia. Fire's just about out. Firemen will take care of that. You might send some coffee out for my men who are staying to watch the horses."

"Absolutely. Anything else?"

"If you have some resort members who know horses, search along the roads at first light, that'd be a help. My men can handle the immediate backcountry. I'll notify the local ranches right away. We'll have plenty of eyes out there." He smiled grimly. "The poor creatures will be wanting a safe place to eat and sleep. Most of them have been at some of the ranches around here for one thing or another."

116

"How can the searchers tell you where they've been? I don't want to waste time searching places twice."

"Just ask the men I'm leaving here. They'll coordinate the search from here. No point looking until dawn."

Mia nodded briskly. "Then I'll go get the coffee. Would some doughnuts as well be too cliché?"

He laughed shortly, resettling his hat at a jauntier angle, badge shining in the firelight. "No, ma'am. But I expect some eggs and bacon would go pretty well with them. Fire fighting is hungry work."

"I'll send a full breakfast out, then." Mia started to leave, then asked, "Please let me know about Becky, Sheriff."

"Yes, ma'am," he agreed, waving an incoming police car to a parking space.

Mia, Atsa, and Sam started the long walk down the road back to the hotel, each lost in their own thoughts. The road seemed to have stretched since they'd run down it just a short time ago. Their feet plodded along, crunching sluggishly in the gravel.

When they got back to the hotel, they went straight to the long wall outside the exhibit hall. No guard stood waiting next to the fire door.

After a brief search, they found the guard. He'd been pulled under a nearby bush, the leaves hiding his prone body. Clever of the thief, Mia thought. It would take that much longer before the crime was discovered. Feeling for his pulse, she was relieved to find his heart beating strongly. His chest rose and fell in a steady rhythm. "Call for another ambulance, Atsa."

"It'll take a few minutes," Atsa told her, squatting beside the guard and checking his pulse herself. "They only have the one. They'll need to drop Becky off and come back."

Mia sighed, "I guess we should go inside and tell the guards the flute has been stolen from under all our noses. And call the police. At least they're already on the grounds."

"I guess," Atsa agreed dully. Her face was streaked with soot and ashes, and her brown eyes were exhausted. "But what about the guard? We can't leave an unconscious man alone, just lying here on the ground."

"I'll stay with him," Sam volunteered.

"Don't let anyone sneak up behind you," Mia warned him as he collapsed on the ground, a second prone figure. "I'd never hear the end of it from your mom."

The guards were not happy, not happy at all. One watched Mia suspiciously as Bob went to check on his fallen comrade. He demanded her identification again while keeping her at a distrustful arm's length, as if Mia had stolen her own flute. Of course, with rampant insurance fraud, he didn't know she hadn't, so she didn't blame him. After radio confirmation with Bob, he unbent enough to allow her to accompany him into the exhibit hall. Sam ran into the hall from the fire door, causing the guard to quickly reach for his weapon.

Mia said, "Sam!" She turned to the guard. "He's with me, one of the hotel employees, and my nephew."

He nodded, still suspicious, tapping in the entry key code. The lights glared on, and the guard cautiously peered into the room. His face paled, and he burst out. "Someone's definitely been in here. A lot of these cases are damaged."

Mia pushed past the stunned guard into the room. She quickly surveyed the room, hands on her hips. All of the valuable displays, carefully locked into their glass cases, had been broken. The carefully labeled plaques were scattered among the shattered glass.

"It looks like the thief chose the very best of everything we had here." Her lips pursed. "Certainly the pieces that will be the most expensive to compensate their owners for."

Sam whistled, "Wow. They've really cleaned us out." He started moving cautiously around the room, feet skittering on glass shards.

"They certainly have," Mia said grimly. She moved into action, calling, "Atsa, take breakfast and coffee to the police, and ask them to please come when they can." She scuffed her foot a little on the glass, watching the light reflect like glittering diamonds. "There's no rush. The thief is long gone with the flute and everything else they stole."

"Um, Aunt Mia," Sam said, staring at something behind the flute's case. "I think there is. Tell them to hurry."

5

A Terrible Tragedy

Mia ventured forward.

Kyle's lifeless body lay sprawled on the floor. A rock hammer that Mia recognized as part of the exhibit lay beside him, its last use obvious from the blood pooling around it, soaking into the wood floor.

Kyle's sleek smugness was gone. All that remained was a horribly broken shell. Black athletic pants twisted around his legs, splayed at unnatural angles. A matching black hoodie covered his torso, but his stomach peeked out, sickly pale beneath the tan and slackened muscles. The hood was thrust back, and that handsome face that had eased Kyle's way through life was no longer handsome.

Feeling a little sick, she stepped back, ordering, "Atsa, make that call right now. There's been a murder."

Atsa ran down the hall, feet slapping the tile floor.

Mia swallowed hard, stomach churning. "Sam, back out slowly and stand next to the guard outside. I expect they'll want to take our shoes for the footprints."

Sam nodded, for once silent. He shoved his hand through his hair, standing it on end. His suddenly very young face reflected his horror and disbelief at sudden death. They stood side by side, exhausted and unsure what to do next. It had been quite a night.

Atsa hurried back, out of breath, black streaks from the fire still marking her face. "The police are on their way." She reassured Mia, "I gave the restaurant instructions to take breakfast to the stable." She choked a little, "I mean the firemen and police," she corrected herself.

"Very good, Atsa," Mia said, her voice deliberately strong, but her legs feeling wobbly beneath her. She abruptly sat down on a chair in the hall.

"Who is it?" Atsa asked.

"Kyle Lee," Mia said shortly.

"Oh no," Atsa exclaimed. After a beat, she asked, "Is there anything I can do?"

"I expect we'll want some of that coffee ourselves after they finish serving the emergency team." Mia sighed, suddenly tired to her bones. "I doubt we'll get to our beds for a while."

"We all have an alibi, at least," Sam said, pacing the hall.

"Sam," Mia remonstrated with a shake of her head.

"Well, it's true," Sam insisted. "I never saw who the first visitor at the fire door was. Did either of you?"

"No, just that someone was there who ran away rather quickly," Mia said.

"I didn't either, just a shape in the dark," Atsa said. She continued practically, "What should I do to keep people out of the crime scene? As soon as guests start coming down, they'll know something is wrong with all the police here."

Mia looked down the hall at the now empty lobby. The two guards carried their fallen comrade inside through the big double doors, ushered in by James, who kept glancing around to make sure no guests popped up in the lobby unexpectedly. Luckily, no guests were here at this hour. They placed the guard gently on the long sofa near the flickering fire. James stood twisting his hands over him, clearly uncertain what to do.

"I honestly don't know, Atsa. What do you think?" she asked, not caring very much about the hotel particulars at the moment.

Collapsing on a nearby chair with his legs sprawled out in front of him, Sam spoke up, "The police can access the exhibit room through the service entrance, right?"

Atsa nodded.

"We're supposed to be having a big party and unveiling tomorrow night," Sam said. "I know that's got to be off after this," he gestured at the closed exhibit doors and searched for a word, "mess, but it will take a while for the guests to know what happened. And don't forget," he reminded them, "a lot of the guests are here just to enjoy the resort. They don't care about exhibits. What they aren't bothered by, they're not going to care about."

"True," Mia agreed. "So what do you propose?"

"A temporary wall at the far end, next to the lobby," Sam suggested. "Just a plain wall, no party coming or balloons. That would be," he screwed his face up, "too weird. If the police agree, maintenance could put that up before most of the guests wake up."

Mia nodded her agreement. "Good thinking, Sam. We'll ask the police. With their permission, Atsa can arrange that."

Atsa added, "I'll call the maintenance people right away. They can be ready to put it up after the police okay it."

Mia thought for a minute. "That's the only safeguard we can do anything about tonight. Tomorrow, we will need to find the stolen exhibits and reschedule the opening party. I think we'll hold it next weekend to allow time for everything to calm down." She mentally planned her next few days.

"Aunt Mia." Sam looked at her, shocked. "Kyle Lee was murdered in the exhibit hall. We can't hold a party there."

"Kyle Lee was wearing all black inside the exhibit hall at a time he had no business being there. It was the middle of the night, and he had wrapped up filming earlier. He was obviously killed by his partner in crime while stealing our flute," she said tartly. "That is not acceptable."

"Well, no," Sam admitted. "But Dad..."

"Your Dad won't be okay with it either." She made a little heartfelt sigh, twisting her pink spinel ring around her finger. "I wish someone besides me would break murder news to Mark for once."

"Someone besides you?" Atsa said, startled. "You've broken murder news before?"

"Oh, you know the hotel business," Mia said vaguely, resettling her sooty scarf around her neck. "There's always something."

"Yes, but murder?" Atsa began.

Mia saw Sam make a shut up and I'll tell you later hand gesture to Atsa, where he thought Mia couldn't see him. She helped by staring vaguely at the opposite wall, twisting her ring around her finger. She wanted a minute to think quietly, not explain things that were already over and done.

Mia had been so sure Kyle was the thief, and now she was equally sure she had been right. There was no other reason for him to be in the exhibit room in the middle of the night unless he was there to steal something.

It now seemed that he'd had a partner in crime as well.

Or, Mia wondered, maybe Kyle had tried to steal the flute the same night as another thief. She turned that possibility around in her mind, slowly considering it from every angle. Was that too much of a coincidence, two different thieves in the same night?

She decided it could have happened. The hammer had been a weapon of opportunity, one found at the exhibit, not brought in with the murderer. Kyle knew the security wouldn't be installed after filming. He'd heard her say so at her dinner party. The reason for the further delay in installing security had been filming was running late. A drink spilled on a laptop by Kyle had been one cause for that delay. Mia felt sure that was only one of multiple delays orchestrated by Kyle, who, after all, was the star of the show. It was hard to film without his cooperation. The security delay could have easily been planned by Kyle.

But while everyone had been checked in and out of the exhibit by the guards, people did gossip. It would have been easy to find out where there was security, and also easy to see where the security guards in their uniforms were stationed. Guests asking about the exhibit wouldn't raise any red flags since many people were here to see the exhibit and attend the opening party and auction. Of course, they would be curious.

The fire at the horse stables was clearly set to distract the guards. And it had worked. Had it been Kyle or another person who set the fire? Someone approached the fire door while they waited to catch a thief, someone scared off by the additional watchers.

Was it Kyle who had crept up, then run away? Had two thieves planned the distraction and theft together? Or had two thieves worked separately, both planning the same ideal night for a heist?

Kyle could have been with his murderer or arrived on his own and surprised another thief into murder. For now, Mia would assume the two thieves worked together. Kyle was certainly annoying enough for someone close to him to murder him.

That narrowed the suspects to people who interacted with Kyle, which should be easy to find in the hotel gossip mill, but she would keep the possibility of two thieves choosing the same night open. Coincidences did happen, and this one wasn't much of a stretch.

Sheriff Hank hurried in, his face covered in grimy sweat from the fire. "I understand there's been a murder here?" His quick eye scanned the room, and he nodded toward the guard lying still, blood streaking his forehead, protectively watched by James. "That one's still alive," he told her bluntly.

"He is indeed," Mia said acidly. "The one in the exhibit room isn't. You know, the exhibit I asked for your help guarding, since I thought there would be a robbery?"

Wisely ignoring her, he hurried down the hallway, returning with his hat off, shaking his head. "When you folks plan an event, you don't cut corners, do you? Arson, assaults, and murder, all in one night. Never heard of such a thing in my county. And you say there's been a theft too?"

"I expect the theft was the reason for the rest of the crimes, Sheriff," Mia said, suddenly exhausted. "Millions of dollars worth of artifacts have been stolen."

"Millions, huh?" He wandered over to the now stirring guard. "Worth that on the open market?"

"I expect it would depend on who is buying, like anything else."

"It usually does." He banged his hat against his leg. "Your son, when he sent you here, didn't have any idea of the thief or the buyers' identities?"

Mia was a little surprised he'd remembered

their brief conversation. "No, he didn't have any other information. Just the thief putting out bids for objects in the exhibit we were holding. I think he said something about the dark web. I know the computer team keeps a close eye on any mention of Spinel Hotels online to forestall potential trouble."

"So what were you doing outside the exhibit tonight?"

Mia told him. His face remained carefully blank, but she saw his mouth twitch. "Okay, you can go. Get some sleep. You look like you could use it," he told her bluntly. He looked at her hard, "Now, don't you go jet-setting off anywhere. I'll need to talk to you tomorrow, too."

"Thank you, sheriff," she replied. "Good night."

She didn't even remember her head hitting the pillow.

6

A Change of Plans

Mia ate breakfast at Mesquite the next morning instead of in her own little courtyard. Everything seemed normal, to her quiet relief. None of the guests appeared aware that anything had happened, thanks to Sam's temporary wall blocking off the hallway. He'd almost redeemed himself from his UFO fiasco with that idea, but Mia wasn't quite ready to let him off the hook. Practical jokes on guests had to be nipped in the bud.

Her omelet, topped with smoky peppers and grilled onions, was the start to the day. As she spread a small concha with prickly pear jelly (unexpectedly delicious), she let her eyes drift around the room.

Neal Mjesec bit with relish into a large buttered muffin with one hand and turned pages in another massive UFO book with the other. Mia considered him for one minute. She had seen no sign of interest in the flute, except as a supposed harbinger of the aliens' arrival. She hadn't seen him plotting with Kyle or showing any interest in the exhibit hall. There weren't any aliens there. On the other hand, UFO hunting was an excellent excuse to turn up in some unexpected places and times. She thought she would keep him in mind, affably harmless as he seemed.

Destiny wolfed down a huge omelet at a nearby table, clearly too hungry to complain about the food. She wore heavy boots and technical clothes and had evidently already been hiking this morning, too, her hair damp with sweat. Mia wished she'd change for the dining room. Dirty boots had no place at any table not covered in a picnic cloth.

Mia noted with mild surprise that Emily was breakfasting alone. Her mousy brown hair was scraped back off her forehead and secured with a limp gray headband. Deep circles shadowed her eyes, and she stirred her food with lackluster interest. Mia supposed the assistant had been so late wrapping up that she was exhausted. Maybe Emily would treat herself to a much-needed vacation after the hectic production. She seemed to be the one organizing the production, despite Mia's initial impression of her ineptitude.

Mia had spotted John and Estela Wallace having breakfast in one of the side alcoves as she came into the restaurant. They ignored Mia, deliberately looking down at their breakfasts to avoid catching her eye. John ordered black coffee on repeat, downing each cup the moment it arrived. Estela toyed with her food, moving her fork around the plate, but not eating much as far as Mia could tell.

She wondered about the couple. John had made no secret of the fact that he'd pay top dollar for the flute. He'd made multiple insistent offers, but he hadn't threatened Mia if she didn't sell it. He'd simply politely upped his offer until the point that the money involved was getting absurd for even a rare artifact. But did that mean John would steal it? Willingness to pay extravagant sums was not the same as willingness to steal. Quite the opposite usually.

They had both appeared to dislike Kyle Lee intensely, with even the extroverted and normally bubbly Estela shrinking away from the archeology host. And Kyle went out of his way to be insulting to them, always just within the bounds of civility. Was it all just an act? Were the Wallaces working with Kyle to steal the flute?

John was rich and used to getting his own way. Mia had the impression the flute was the first thing in a long time that he wanted but couldn't get. At some point, most men would have shrugged their shoulders and decided to get some other prize for their collection. John was still upping his price to the point that even Mia was a little tempted. If the flute hadn't been so clearly a treasure belonging to the nation, she would certainly have sold it.

In their little alcove, John and Estela remained deep in conversation, wrapped up in their own world. Did they know there had been a theft yet, or was John planning other methods to purchase the flute? Why did Estela look so upset, especially if she didn't know there had been a murder? Had someone told them about the murder already?

Or did John break into the exhibit room by himself, taking advantage of the security he knew was lax? After all, it was doubtful Mia would prosecute if he was caught, since it would be dreadful for hotel's public relations. Maybe John had run into Kyle Lee there and grabbed the first object to silence him that came to hand. Anything was possible, Mia thought. Most of the very rich hired people to do their dirty work. Would John have hired Kyle or just done it himself? John was a hands-on owner of his oil company, judging by the stories circulating about him. A hired thief was also a potential blackmailer. Mia didn't think John would have taken that chance unless he had distanced himself from potential blackmail.

Kyle would have made an excellent blackmailer, too. Hmm. Mia set her coffee down and rose. She deliberately went over to the Wallaces' table. "Good morning, John, Estela." Estela's beautiful brown eyes were red-rimmed from hours of tears. The couple were clearly not in the mood to casually chat over breakfast.

But Mia was a little difficult to ignore, standing there. John recovered first. "Mia! Good morning! We'd ask you to join us, but—" He gestured insincerely at the lack of a chair.

"Thank you for the thought, John, but I just finished my own breakfast," she told them. "I wanted to tell you some news before you heard it anywhere else."

"Yes?" John said noncommittally.

"The exhibit was robbed last night." She ignored Estela's quick intake of breath. "And Kyle Lee was found dead, murdered, in the room."

"Kyle dead? Murdered?" Estela's voice rose in a high screech. "This can not be! Not here, of all places! Not near me!" Heads turned. Mia gave an inward shrug. It wasn't as if the news wouldn't carry the story of a murder. Murder at your hotel wasn't something that could be hidden for long, no matter how insulated your vacation was. Estela made little sobbing sounds, squeaky and forlorn.

John shoved back his chair, "Back to the cottage, sweetheart." He grabbed her elbow, trying to get her to rise.

"But I want to know," Estela protested, breath coming in jerky spasms.

"Mia will come along with us, won't you?" He glared an order at Mia. "Let's get out of here. You're making a scene, honey."

Mia took Estela's other elbow, and together they steered her back to her cottage, unsteadily teetering on her strappy Manolo Blahnik sandals and choking incoherent questions.

The Wallaces were staying in one of the larger cottages, not far from Mia's. The adobe building had just the right amount of luxury, with soft woven blankets, intricately painted tiled floor, and a magnificent view of the mountains. They settled Estela in a big, comfortable chair, legs propped on a footstool. She impatiently took off her shoes. Red marks encircled her ankles where the straps had bitten in. John tenderly wrapped a blanket around his wife, then thumped into a nearby chair.

"So what happened?" he demanded.

"Someone broke into the exhibit hall, stole the flute and a few other artifacts, and killed Kyle Lee in the exhibit hall," Mia stated bluntly.

"Any of my stuff?"

"At least one piece I noticed—that exquisite little corrugated bowl, but I haven't done a full inventory yet," Mia told him. "The police were in charge, obviously."

John grunted, "Nice piece, hate to lose it, but I have other similar ones. Otherwise, I wouldn't have lent it. But the flute..." He rapped sharply on a nearby table. "What happened?"

"The security system couldn't be installed as planned because the filming ran very late yesterday. So I had a guard on the outside door, two on the public hall, and two on the service hallway." She smiled a little ruefully, "I was concerned about the outside fire door being a weak point, so my nephew, a team member, and I supplemented the outside guard."

"More to the point if you'd sat inside and stared at the flute all night," John growled.

Mia returned dryly, "That was unfortunately against the insurance policy, so I covered the entrances instead. The cases were locked and had alarms."

Estela gasped, finally seeming to hear the conversation. "John! Kyle was killed in the exhibit. Mia is lucky she is not hurt. She acted bravely to guard it at all, out there at night."

He backed down a little. "True. Can I assume you didn't stand there all night then?"

"Someone set fire to the stables," Mia told him.

"An obvious distraction," he bluntly stated.

"Naturally," Mia agreed. "But the horses still had to get out of the burning stable, and we were the closest available."

John nodded reluctantly.

"Did you get the poor things out?" Estella asked with concern, struggling a little to get out of her tightly wrapped blanket.

"Every one of them," Mia reassured her. "We left the guard outside the windows, but that was a big area for one man to cover." She shook her head, unsure what other choice she could have made. "While we were gone, someone hit the guard over the head, opened the door, and stole the flute."

"And my bowl. Then killed Kyle for good measure," John stated. "Busy night for someone."

"Yes," Mia agreed, feeling exhausted still.

"The stables?" Estela seemed to be coming to life again. "Is Becky okay? I know she had been sleeping out there to protect the horses." She told John, "Someone has been borrowing them at night, and they come back worn out. She was so upset." She shook her head sorrowfully.

"Becky is fine, but she was hit over the head by whoever set the fire. The last I heard, she was going to the hospital to be checked out, protesting all the way." Mia paused, "I didn't know you knew Becky?"

"She took me trail riding a few times, and we've worked together on a children's charity," Estela explained absently. "She is very nice and so good with helping the children to ride. I am glad she is okay." She shook her head sadly. "She told me about the horses being ridden at night because Missy, that is the one I like to ride, was one of them. Poor girl. She was too tired to ride last time." She looked down at the blanket, stroking the soft wool.

"I think Becky will be fine since we got all the horses out. That was really what worried her. She's in the hospital now, but just for observation after her head injury. I'll tell you when I know more, if you would like?"

"Yes, please," she knit her brows together in a frown. "How was Kyle killed?" Estela asked, twisting her blanket fringe around one delicate finger.

"He was hit over the head with a rock hammer that was part of the exhibit," Mia said with distaste.

"Anyone could use a hammer to kill someone. It would be easy," Estela said thoughtfully, twining the fringe around and around her manicured nails.

"Honey, don't say things like that," John ordered her. He growled, "Kyle couldn't even die without causing more trouble."

"They will say I did it." She gulped in air, big tears suddenly running down her face. "I hated him, and now he is dead. Why did this have to happen?"

"Be quiet!" John's voice was harsh, but his big hands were gentle as he patted her shoulder.

"Estela, if it's public knowledge you hated Kyle, I'd tell the sheriff. He seems like a decent man. If it's not public knowledge, don't say a word to anyone, not even me." She smiled to take any sting out of her words. Mia knew that was the right thing to say, and she would find out either way. There were very few real secrets in any community, and the Wallaces were prominent citizens.

"Oh!" Estela said, covering her face, then lowered the blanket to reveal tears. "It is public, Mia, very public. It is just a very long time ago. I was such a child then." Her exquisitely sculpted face turned to Mia in supplication.

"Kyle stole artifacts from Estela's family in Mexico," John explained shortly. "Some pots, jewelry, things they had found on their land. Kyle tried to peddle them to me. I found out where they came from and returned them to Estela's family."

"And John and I met," Estela said, looking at him with adoring, tear-filled eyes. She told Mia, "My father heard noises in the middle of the night. He went down to investigate alone. The study, where he displayed all the beautiful things our family had found on our land, had nothing left but bare shelves. All our family treasures. He collapsed in a heart attack. I found him there in the morning." Her mouth tightened in memory.

"Oh no!" Mia was shocked.

"He came through okay," Estella shrugged her beautiful shoulders, "but he has never been as healthy as he was before Kyle robbed us."

"Did you prosecute him?"

She shivered, holding up her hands. "I was so young, I had imagined I was in love with Kyle." She shook her head, mouth pursed, disgusted at her past self. "We were engaged, the wedding announced. My father trusted Kyle, let him in our house, let him see what we had there. It was all my fault." She gulped back a sob. "Kyle threatened to tell the police my father was dealing drugs."

"That police department, they seize your land and throw you in jail, then ask their questions," John said.

"With my father so sick, in the hospital for so long, we could not take the chance." Estela spread her hands helplessly. "John returned everything back to my family, but Kyle got away with his theft."

John patted her shoulder. "At least I got the best thing in my life out of it."

"And I, too." She held his hand for a minute and smiled up at him through her tears, wiping them away. "My poor father, though. I hated Kyle for that."

"I wish you had told me," Mia said with chagrin. "I would never have had him as the presenter." She felt terrible for exposing Estela to that predator again.

"I know, Mia," Estela told her, reaching out her hand to pat Mia's, "but by the time we found out, he had already started work on the program. To cancel would have caused the nasty scandal to all come up again, maybe reporters harassing my father this time. I decided to simply ignore Kyle." She smiled at her husband, "I knew John would not let him bother me."

"From Richard's reactions, I knew he wouldn't let Kyle anywhere near the museum or flute after the film was finished," John said.

"Richard made it clear he didn't have a very high opinion of Kyle, didn't he?" Mia commented. "He told me Kyle had tried to steal a South African national treasure, an ancient human skull, on one documentary."

"Oh no," Estela said. "So it was more than just my family he stole from?"

"It seems that many documentaries he worked on missed valuable objects," Mia agreed.

"So I guess it's pretty clear what little Kyle was doing in the exhibit hall last night. He was after the flute," John stated. "I'll bet he was all decked out in cat burglar black, too."

Mia nodded in agreement. "He was indeed. Head to toe black, even a hoodie."

John sniggered, an odd sound from such a large man.

"The question is, did he bring his killer to the exhibit or just meet him there?" Mia asked.

They were quiet for a minute. "It could have been either," Estela finally said, smoothing her blanket thoughtfully.

"Yes," Mia rose to go. "Estela, I wouldn't say anything to the sheriff unless he asks you."

She looked up at Mia, long lashes still wet with tears. "Do you think?"

"I think so. It was a long time ago. He probably had more recent victims," Mia said. "But, I'm sorry I have to ask, did Kyle work with anyone else when he," she stumbled for a word, "stole from your family?"

"He was in Mexico, filming a documentary at a nearby archeological site," Estela said with a grimace, clearly forcing herself to think about those days. "I suppose all his crew were there. I did not really meet them so much. The same director as here, Hal Abrams, I think. I know he always used the same head cameraman back then, but I don't know if that's still true." She shrugged her beautiful shoulders in a graceful arc. "It was such a long time ago. Another lifetime for me." She pushed the blanket back off her shoulders and sat up a little, crossing her legs and positioning them carefully for the optimal angle of attractiveness, just as a matter of habit. "I really did not mix with his crew. My father would not have allowed it."

"I'll tell the sheriff to talk to both Richard and his cameraman. Pete was with Kyle on that South African trip. The skull fossil was actually found in Pete's camera bag. It was sheer luck Pete didn't end up in a South African prison."

"Oh no," Estela exclaimed.

"That makes Pete the right person to break the news to the sheriff that Kyle was a suspected thief. Kyle had been in that game for a while, so he'd have contacts in the criminal world as well."

"Contacts that may have killed him?" John asked. "That would make the most sense. He had to sell the loot to someone." He patted Estela's tanned leg and stood up, clearly wanting Mia to leave now she'd answered all his questions. "I know the police will do their best to get my bowl and anything else missing back, Mia, but if they don't find it, the hotel will be responsible for my loss, you know." He spoke slightly diffidently for him, visibly trying not to offend her with his normal blunt style.

Mia quickly assured him, "Naturally, John. But we will recover the stolen pieces."

"You think so?" he asked, disbelieving.

"I do," she stated with the utmost confidence. "There is only one road in or out of the hotel," she held up one finger and nodded, "and the police have had it blocked almost since the theft took place. Artifacts aren't leaving by the road anytime soon, and no hotel guests are missing."

"What about trails out?"

"The horses are well guarded, considering what happened, and the hotel trail toys are locked under normal circumstances. I checked this morning, and currently they're under police guard. It's a long way to hike out through the desert." Mia shuddered inwardly at the long, dry hike through rocky desert terrain. Her mouth felt dry at the thought. She reassured John, "There is simply not a way off the hotel grounds where a thief won't be seen, so keep an eye out for our artifacts. They have to be on the hotel grounds."

"Will do," John said, clearly feeling slightly more optimistic. His eyes became thoughtful.

"You two just relax today," Mia said. "Enjoy the spa, Estela. It's on me."

She smiled, her red, curved mouth relaxing. "I might do that."

Mia thought she might try out the spa too. A little relaxation sounded perfect. But first, she had to talk to the hotel manager.

At this late hour, Don Lagarto had obviously just arrived at work. He sat at his desk, planted like a huge sluggish toad, being briefed by Atsa. Shifting from one foot to another, Atsa looked exasperated. She turned to Mia with relief. "Ms. Mia, maybe you can tell Mr. Lagarto all about last night's events. I should get back to the front desk."

"Of course, Atsa." Mia asked the manager, "What would you like to know?"

"There was really a murder in my hotel last night?" Don Lagarto asked in disbelief.

"Yes, and a theft of some very valuable artifacts." Mia mentally added, the objects I was assured would have an active security system on them.

"I tell you, no one cares about the damn rocks. But a murder, that's another story." He threw his hands up in the air and compressed his fleshy lips. "We'll shut down the hotel immediately."

"Excuse me?"

"The hotel must be shut down right now. One of our guests is probably the killer. We have to kick them all out of the hotel." He picked up the phone, presumably to do just that.

Mia, shocked, took the phone out of his hand. "Absolutely not."

"I'm the manager of this hotel. We can't have a killer going around murdering everyone in the hotel. So I'm kicking the murderer and everyone else out and shutting down the hotel. No more deaths." He tried to grab the phone back.

"I am the owner of this hotel, and I am telling

you we are not shutting it down."

He quit trying to grab the phone from Mia. She was faster than he was. "We should kick them out," he repeated sullenly, staring down at his cluttered desk.

"They are our guests, staying at our hotel. We will do our best to make sure the murder and theft," she emphasized the word, "affect their stays as little as possible."

"How could it not? The police..."

"Will only question guests who had contact with the exhibit or the victim. The theft of the valuable flute was obviously the reason for the murder. If you had installed the security as you told me you would, this would never have happened." She went on with asperity, "I am surprised you weren't at the hotel after the stable fire."

"Who cares if the stable burned down? The builders probably set a fire on purpose to get more work," he moved his pudgy shoulders uncomfortably. "How was I supposed to know anyone would steal old rocks?"

Mia gritted her teeth and said nothing. There was no point.

"I'm leaving in an hour anyway. So it's your problem. You brought the exhibit here. Your problem," he stated.

"What?"

He wiggled into his chair, getting comfortable. "My brother and I have tickets to the baseball game this afternoon. I can't disappoint my brother. He's had these tickets a long time."

"But you're the manager! You can't just leave when there's a crisis happening. It's your job to manage crises." As a hotel manager, Mia had worked all hours and all jobs during emergencies. It was part of the job.

"Hey, my solution is to kick out all the guests, so there's no crisis. If they're all gone, no more murders in the hotel." He spread his pudgy hands in sluggish supplication. "You said no. So it's your problem now."

Mia didn't trust herself to speak. Instead, she turned and left the room. She stopped at the concierge desk. "Atsa, please instruct my hospitality team to ignore any orders the manager gives."

She tossed back her long black braid, "Like what?"

"He wanted to close the hotel."

Atsa's mouth rounded in a long whistle. "No."

"We will not be doing that," Mia said with decision, eyes narrowed in anger. "He will be leaving for a baseball game soon and will not be here to cause problems. I will let Mark deal with him when he has a chance." Her mouth flattened in a tight line. "I feel sure he will make time."

"I totally understand," Atsa said, amusement in her voice. "I'll alert the rest of the team if necessary." Her smile grew wider. "He doesn't usually bother giving many orders, so people would wonder if he did tell them to do anything much."

Mia wondered again who actually ran the hotel. Her guess was all the hospitality team, excepting the manager. "If there are any managerial decisions to be made, please tell me, and I will handle them."

Atsa nodded, smiling. "Will do."

Growling like a frustrated bear, Destiny stormed the front desk, wildly flailing a hand-embroidered bag, contents straining at the seams. Obviously furious, her turquoise beads clacking with agitation, she accused, "I can't get into the Spirit Guide room. It's locked and has this sign on it." She waved the improvised sign she'd clearly ripped off the door under Atsa's nose, hand shaking in anger.

Atsa masterfully fielded the implied question without backing away, "I'm sorry, the spirit guide room is closed for some much-needed renovations."

"Renovations? Now?" Destiny's long, narrow face reddened with anger. Her beads rattled, and her eyes narrowed. She shook her fist at Atsa. "I need to get into that room. Immediately." She whipped a smudge stick out of the bag. Mia noticed the bag struggled to hold her ample supply, lined up around the sides like ammunition. "I need to smudge the room to keep the spirits from getting angry. There's been a murder!" Her voice rose to a screech that the entire room heard.

Aware of the lobby audience, Mia decided to step in. "Destiny, is it? I'm one of the new hotel owners, Mia Spinel." She continued, "We're renovating the entire hotel, including the spirit guide room."

"But I need to do my meditation in there. That's the only place it works." She waved the smudge stick wildly around her like a grenade with the pin out.

Mia said, with all the sympathy she could contrive after Destiny's mediation cacophony last night, "I'm sorry, but we scheduled the renovation crews some

time out, and the room very much needs a refresh."
That was an outright lie, but they'd be renovating that
room out of existence as soon as she could arrange it.

"But after the murder, I need to smudge that
room," Destiny was almost howling in frustration. Her
red-rimmed eyes were painful in their panic. "The
spirits listen to me there!"

Mia saw everyone in the lobby whipping their
heads around at the word "murder." People weren't just
casually overhearing an obnoxious guest now; they were
overtly trying to hear what was going on. Well, that's
done it, Mia thought. Anyone who hadn't heard about
the murder would hear all about it now.

She suggested evenly, "Several outdoor
meditation areas are available. There's a particularly
serene one with a beautiful mountain view. Here's the
hotel map with all the locations marked." Her icy tone
was of finality.

She held out the map, and Destiny slapped it
back on the desk. "Like I need a map!" she scoffed.

Destiny stood still a moment, aggressively
forlorn, her shoulders slumped in her expensive, trendy
yoga clothes. "I'll think of something," she said bitterly,
shoving the wrapped bundles of sage back in her bag
with clumsy, tangerine orange-nailed fingers. "If there's
another murder, it's all your fault!" she told Mia. She
strode off toward the guest rooms.

Atsa nodded in wholehearted approval, braid
swinging. "It's about time that awful room was fixed.
I'm all for spiritual activities, but that room was
obnoxiously loud next to the lobby, and it's like a

museum of the worst of hoodoo. Guests are coming to me with so many questions; I just didn't know how to answer. Aunt Chooli hates it, says it's a disgrace to the spirits." She smiled as two boys ran up to the front desk.

"That woman said there was a murder!" they burst out breathlessly.

The taller boy asked, voice piercing with excitement, "Can we see the body?"

"We've never seen a real dead body," the other added, eager eyes wide. "Just in movies." They clearly thought the murder had been arranged for their entertainment.

Mia sighed inwardly. "The police took away the body, so you can't see it," she told them. She added at a level calculated to carry distinctly to the entire lobby, "The murder was committed during a theft at the upcoming museum exhibit. The police are present, but the murder is connected with the exhibit, not the hotel. One of the documentary production employees was sadly killed during the theft. They removed the body last night, soon after the murder and theft were discovered." Heads turned away, discussing the news. The volume in the room rose.

"That's totally unfair! How can we investigate the murder if we can't see the body?" The boys returned to their parents, expressions glum.

Mia looked after them for a minute and sighed. She wished she felt like murder was an adventure, not a tragedy of human life and greed. "Are you getting a lot of questions about the murder?"

"Not too many yet, but I'm sure we will now," Atsa said, looking around the lobby. "There's no way hotel guests will ignore it completely." She shrugged, "I emphasize Kyle's connection to the production, not the hotel."

"Good," Mia left as an anxious couple came up.

As Mia walked down the service hallway, she ran into Susan, looking completely frazzled. Her clipboard hung by her side, and her all-black outfit was wrinkled with a coffee stain dripping down the blouse. "Ms. Mia, I just heard! What can we do? The exhibit is ruined!"

Mia reassured her, "Susan, we will simply postpone the exhibit until next weekend. Everything will continue just like we planned, from there."

"But the flute was stolen!" Susan said, face crumpling into tears. "There's no point in an exhibit now."

"The police are working hard on the case," Mia said. "I'm sure they'll have it back soon." They will if I have anything to do with it, she thought.

"What if next weekend is full? The room could be booked," Susan worried.

"The exhibit was running through the month, so we're fine," Mia told her. "Just plan on the party next weekend."

"What about all the food ordered for tonight? It's a lot of food to waste." She tapped her clipboard as if she could conjure an answer.

"Why don't you organize a free buffet for tonight? Create a really fun event that will wipe the murder off everyone's minds. Announce it around the hotel."

Susan's anxiety dissipated slightly. "Okay, I can do that. Free food always relaxes people. How about at the pool? Maybe some party games too? Make the weekend really fun." She scribbled a note on a fresh sheet and tapped her pen definitively. A smile grew on her face. "That will be easy to pull together since we'd already planned the party."

"Good," Mia said. "I'll tell Chef Chooli we're moving the exhibit event until next weekend and about the buffet tonight. Go ahead and make signs for the event. I think you're right, poolside is nicely removed from recent problems." She enthused, "We'll turn this weekend back into a fun event for our guests."

Susan wrote, "Announcements" on her clipboard.

"Oh, and Susan, the black looks very nice, but don't forget to sponge off your blouse."

Susan quickly looked down and colored, "When I heard the news, I spilled my coffee. I just forgot." She brushed at it ineffectually.

"Absolutely understandable. At least coffee sponges off easily," Mia agreed, quickly finishing the conversation with, "I think a pool party will have our guests enjoying their stay at the hotel, rather than associating it with a murder."

Susan smiled with determination, scribbling on her clipboard. "I'm going to make it an event to remember." She hurried off, happy to have a task to perform.

As Mia continued down the service hallway, she heard muffled shouts. As she opened Mesquite's kitchen door, the yelling became louder.

Destiny's hands each held a smudge stick, and she yelled like a banshee. Smoke streamed around the kitchen as she waved them around like she was marshaling an airplane down the runway. The restaurant team coughed at the acrid smoke while watching the show, grins on their faces. "A murder has poisoned this hotel. I'm not letting the bad energy from that near my food. Everyone should leave while I'm smudging the room. I don't want anyone's bad energy to mess things up more." She waved the smoldering sticks wildly, and smoke streamed through the air.

Mia said with alarm, "Destiny, what are you doing here? Guests aren't allowed in the kitchen."

"It's the closest I can get to the spirit guide room with your stupid renovations," Destiny hissed at her and waved smoke in Mia's face. "The spirits will hear me in here."

The fire alarm went off, adding loud, insistent cries to the noise. The kitchen team stood gaping at the invader, ignoring the alarm as small entertainment value compared to what Destiny was providing.

"I'm protecting the hotel from spiritual damage. The spirits will listen to me and help find Kyle's killer." Destiny added prosaically, "And I need more sage to smudge the entire hotel, so I came to the kitchen to get it."

One of the crew commented helpfully, "I think it's white sage you need, not cooking sage. They're not the same thing."

"It's better than nothing," Destiny waved the smudge sticks wildly, losing one in a soapy sink. She almost grabbed for it, then realized it was soaking wet anyway. "I'm trying to save you idiots." She waved her remaining stick menacingly at Mia, who adroitly stepped back a foot, away from the sooty stick.

Deciding this had gone on long enough, Mia said, "Stop," in a penetrating voice and hit a large hanging pot with a spoon. It rang like a gong, reverberating through the kitchen.

The noise startled Destiny enough to turn and look at her. The room fell into complete silence except for the shrill, insistent beep of the smoke alarm. She continued, "This is not the time or place for smudging. Having a burning stick waving around inside the hotel is clearly against fire code, so put it out. Now." She glared up at Destiny, forcing her to back down.

"I'm just trying to help," Destiny muttered. She dropped the remaining stick in the sink with the other. One woman hurried over and turned the sink on full to put the sooty smoke out.

"As a guest and not an employee of this hotel, you need to remain in the public, guest areas of the hotel from now on." Mia added, "I believe there is a spiritual guidance class with smudging every morning in the Labyrinth."

"Like I need spiritual guidance. I know what I'm doing," Destiny rejoined. "I've been coming here forever. I always go in the kitchen. Right, Chooli?"

Mia saw the head chef, a round little woman in

a black dress and sparkling white apron, roll her large, expressive eyes at the ceiling. "She always does." She tossed a huge hunk of dough onto the long wooden table with a loud thunk.

"What you've done in the past is not important," Mia told Destiny. "This hotel is under new ownership, and guests are not allowed in the service-only areas. And we can't have smudging inside the hotel for any reason whatsoever. Let me escort you out."

"Don't bother." Destiny slammed open the door to the restaurant proper, almost knocking down a waiter entering the other side.

Mia told Chef Chooli respectfully, "You never have to have any guests in your kitchen uninvited. She has no business smoking up the room."

"Yes, yes, Ms. Mia. Destiny is difficult to contain, as always." The tiny, round woman, a full head shorter than Mia, precisely placed a stick of wood into the fireplace dominating the kitchen. The fireplace was round, covered with clay, and resembled a hearth in a primitive adobe hut. The flames burned low on its massive stone slab hearth. A large carved wooden table sat nearby, mounded high with dough. Chef Chooli expertly rolled out a tortilla, perfectly round, and tossed it into the mouth of the fire. With plump, bare hands, she deftly pulled it back after just a minute, stuck a little clay spoon into a cast iron pot simmering on the side of the fire, and spooned a charred pepper mixture onto the center, folded it, and handed it to Mia. "Eat this, girl. You'll feel better. You had an unusual time last night." She turned back to her hearth.

Mia ate, her breathing deliberately slowing as she ate. You never argued with a chef in her kitchen, and it had been a very long time since she'd been called a girl. "Delicious, Chef. Thank you." She smiled, her peace restored. The kitchen gradually returned to the usual bustle of a hotel kitchen.

Mia stood a moment in the center of the room, taking in the kitchen. It was unlike any hotel kitchen she had ever been in, and she had seen a few. The fireplace, and probably the room as well, was obviously part of the original construction of the ranch, the adobe chimney disappearing into the ceiling with most of the smoke. Plastered walls were painted with bright Pueblo motifs in geometric zigzags and triangles. Huge wooden beams crossed the ceiling, festooned with drying herbs and braided onions. Bundles of lemons and limes hung gathered in string bags around the wall, ready for use. The dimly lit room had long, low windows on one side, slivers of light illuminating the cool, dark room. The kitchen was quiet, unbelievably quiet for a restaurant kitchen, just the sounds of knives chopping on wooden cutting boards and wooden spoons stirring bright ceramic bowls, no whirring of mixers and harsh dings on metal tables. A chef pounded with a wooden mortar and pestle, adding more spice and salt to their mixture as he tasted it. Glass jars with unidentifiable contents and handwritten labels were arranged on wooden shelves around the room.

A dishwashing alcove with up-to-date

sanitizing dishwashers was the only concession to a normal restaurant kitchen. The modern machines glared out at the rest of the room, clearly belonging to a different world. A few doorways off the sides presumably led to refrigeration rooms, but they didn't intrude on the primitive kitchen.

Mia stood for a minute, just watching Chef Chooli Biakeddy cook. She bustled around the kitchen, an ancient, round woman in a black dress, ruling her kitchen, like so many women wearing black dresses and aprons around the world ruled their households. The atmosphere was of a matriarch of the family directing preparations for an important holiday feast. She moved through the room like a bouncing ball, tasting, adding spices, showing a young employee exactly how she wanted carrots chopped, and generally making certain everything was done to her standards. In her wake, peaceful action reigned.

The ancient dance of a woman in her kitchen, cooking up wonderful things. It was a shock to realize this woman was a world-famous chef whose cooking drew people to this hotel from around the world. Mia now understood why the food at Mesquite was so unusual. It had been cooked the same way women cooked food for a hundred, for a thousand years. The recipes had been perfected by generations of the Biakeddy women. The meals were just shared with a larger group of guests now. This kitchen was the heart of the hotel.

Reluctantly, Mia left the kitchen, feeling like she had been transported back a thousand years and returned with a harsh thump to her own time. The hospitality team hall was too bright, too glaringly white after the warmly lit kitchen. There was no softly lit charm or flickering firelight here in the modern world. Giving herself a slight shake, she looked in the door leading to the exhibit room.

A policeman was standing at the entrance to the room, clearly placed there to discourage sightseers. "Ma'am? You can't go in there." His body blocked the doorway.

"Of course not," Mia acquiesced, hiding her disappointment. "I'm one of the hotel owners. I just wanted to know if there was anything the sheriff needs."

"Hold on." He turned, then ordered her, "Stay right there."

There wasn't much she could see from the doorway since a room divider blocked the view. She waited patiently, trying not to crane her neck to see what was going on in the room too obviously.

After a few minutes, the sheriff came up. "How's Becky?" She asked the question she most wanted to know.

He nodded in greeting. "Miss Rebecca's staying another night in the hospital. Quite a knock she got on her head, but she'll be just fine. Your guard will be all right, too. He didn't see a dang thing, knocked out from behind."

With a slight grin, he added, "The doc there is a friend of mine. I asked him to keep Miz Rebecca there an extra day so she wouldn't be chasing after those horses. She wouldn't be home an hour before she was after them. We're going to have to hog tie her to the hospital bed soon."

"That does sound like her," Mia agreed.

"We're down to one missing horse, Lightning. He hasn't shown up at any of the obvious places," the sheriff said. "Just like him, that is."

"He seemed a little difficult." Mia wondered what a spirited horse was doing at a resort stable.

Hank nodded, reading her mind. "She rescued him a few months back. He'll be right in time. Miz Rebecca always does have a soft spot for the ornery ones." He tipped his hat back and grinned. "Guess that's why she puts up with me."

Mia grinned back at him, "She seems like a very special woman."

Sheriff Hank coughed. "Well, now, I'd better get back to this here investigation. Anything else you want to know?"

"I did wonder if you were closer to finding out what happened?"

"Nope. Hope we find a clue in this room." He frowned, "There is one odd thing."

"Yes?"

"I'm not sure the thief left by way of the fire door. The footprints are all mixed up, but it looks like the door was closed off after entry and the alarm didn't go off. Do you know of another way out of this room?"

Mia looked around the large exhibit hall, thinking. It had been renovated, probably carved from an actual ballroom in ages past. The room was a simple, large box lined in age darkened wood panels. The upper level had ornate balconies cantilevered over the floor. She thought with a smile, once chaperons, dressed in their finest, must have sat and gossiped at the younger generation dancing below them. However, she had noticed on her tour of the upper hallway that the balconies were firmly shut off from intruders, with panels locked in place. She didn't see any other exits from the room. "Did the guards in the service hall leave during the fire?"

"Yeah, they went outside to check that the fire was under control. Fire's a serious danger out here." He shrugged. "The alarm went off, and they both ran out to see. Not the brightest bulbs you've got there."

"Well, we ran for it too when we heard the horses," Mia said with a shrug. "So the thief may have escaped outside, back the way he came, or escaped through this door." She looked at the large service door. There just aren't any other exits."

"I guess so," Sheriff Hank agreed.

"If they came through the service entrance, that makes it likely the thief is a hotel guest or employee," she continued the thought. "Of course, security is designed to prevent unauthorized people from coming into the hospitality team areas, not leaving them."

"No vehicles left by the road during that time. A lot came in, but no one left until the ambulance went out, and I'm damn sure they didn't stop long enough for anyone else to hitch a ride." He sighed, his blue eyes a little dim.

"Could anyone have left the hotel grounds after

the murder discovery?"

"Not by the road. We've been checking every car going out since we knew there was a murder. Ain't no murdering horse thieving varmint getting millions of dollars of loot past us." He looked at her, his bright blue eyes suddenly sharp, "Of course, there's more ways than roads."

"Perhaps someone who scouted horse trails beforehand?" Mia asked. "With borrowed horses?"

"Maybe," he drew out the word, considering it slowly. "And maybe that was a bunch of kids playing games that didn't know no better. Horses all accounted for but Lightning, like I said. Ain't no one casually hopping on him for a joyride, either. All guests and hospitality team are accounted for. If anyone left the immediate hotel area, they weren't gone for long. I'm pretty sure the loot is still on the hotel grounds." He resettled his hat. "Keep this under your hat, but I want you to be on the lookout for anything odd." He looked hard at her, "I also want you to remember, this person hits people over the head and don't care if they die. So come to me with anything you hear."

"Of course," Mia nodded agreement. "I did want to advise you to talk with Kyle Lee's cameraman, Pete. I'm afraid I don't know his last name. Pete has a story about Kyle possibly stealing while on another production."

He looked quizzically at her, but only said, "Will do."

"Do your men need coffee or anything else?"

"I think we're good. Atsa brought us an urn.

They've been keeping it full." He grinned, sun-tanned skin crinkling around tired blue eyes. "If I drink much more coffee, I'll get the jitters."

"We can't have that," Mia said. "I'll leave you to it, then. Good luck."

On her way out, Mia paused by the front desk, contemplating her next move. Atsa looked up and smiled. The lack of sleep hadn't affected her bright eyes at all. "What next?" she asked, eager to be in on the next adventure.

Mia said slowly, "I don't think I've seen enough of this hotel. I've spent most of my time working on the exhibit. Is there somewhere I could get a good view of the entire resort, maybe an overlook?"

"There's a gorgeous place where you can see the entire hotel grounds, right next to the flute dig site. It's pretty far off the beaten track, though." Atsa suggested, "Why don't you let Sam take you? I know he's guided hikes on Deer Canyon trail, so he knows most of the area around the hotel. The road to the overlook branches off from that. He can take you to see the new observatory site, too."

When Mia found Sam, he was chatting with a very pretty guest by the pool. Her bright pink bikini unsurprisingly didn't leave much to the imagination, but Mia was disconcerted when she overheard a snippet of their unlikely conversation about the geology of some of the desert rock formations. Sam, as well as his companion, had hidden depths, it seemed.

Smiling, she cleared her throat slightly, and Sam jumped off the girl's pool lounger with a slightly embarrassed look. "Hi, Aunt Mia!" he greeted her with exaggerated enthusiasm.

"Hello, Sam. May I speak with you for a minute?" She smiled at the guest.

"Sure," he leaned toward the girl, smiling. "See you tonight!"

She smiled back, opening her book, a geology tome. Sam followed Mia, looking back at the pretty girl with a wave.

"Sam, I'm sorry to disturb you in your time off, but Atsa told me there's a good hotel overlook next to the dig site. I'd like to see the entire grounds. Can you guide me out to it?"

"No problem," he said enthusiastically. "It's not far at all. You'll love it, really epic view."

"And Sam? We do want to keep the recent upsets as quiet as possible."

"Of course. You don't have to tell me that, Aunt Mia," he told her with a hurt expression.

"Thank you, Sam. I'll meet you after lunch, then."

Giving a studiously casual wave back at the girl, Sam strode off purposefully.

Mia went back to her room to change into clothes she could hike in. She enjoyed a lunch of squash soup and smoked trout sandwiches delivered to her little courtyard, while looking warily at the distant mountains she'd be hiking up soon. She hoped going up to the overlook wouldn't be too strenuous a hike. She still felt a little tired after last night.

7

The Eagle's Aerie

Sam met her in the lobby, grinning from ear to ear. "Wait until you see this, Aunt Mia! You're going to love it!"

He gestured dramatically at a truncated car with a roll cage, deeply treaded tires, and bright red paint. "Ta da!" He beamed at his aunt, proud of his ingenuity.

"A dune buggy? Sam, I don't know..."

"A side-by-side, not a dune buggy! It'll be perfect for exploring a much larger area than us going in on foot. You won't even have to hike a step." He slid into the seat and clipped his safety belt on. Revving the engine to a roar, he handed her a bright orange helmet with a flourish. "Hotel regulations, we have to wear them."

Mia looked at her perfectly broken-in Zamberlan hiking boots with a twinge of disappointment. She'd been looking forward to a nice, quiet hike through the desert, even if the mountains looked a little daunting at the moment. She always thought problems through best on walks. With an inward sigh, she fitted the bulky helmet on and eased into the bucket seat, cinching her seatbelt tight. Sam revved the engine with a roar, and they were off, bouncing down a dirt road barely distinguishable from the surrounding desert.

They had no trouble finding the road to the new observatory, since construction passed on it frequently. "Here it is," Sam yelled over the noise of the engine. "We'll go past the observatory site and on to the original dig site. It's a little further up the mountain. Look for clues!"

Mia wondered how clues could be spotted while racing through the desert, but she could always return later for closer inspection, now that she knew where to go. Sam's grin was infectious, and she was starting to enjoy the bumpy drive. Traveling so fast and so close to the rocky terrain took a little getting used to, but it was fun to drive racketing along the trail.

Deer Canyon Trail was a wide dirt road, deeply rutted by construction trucks—ideal for shepherding a large hiking group or driving a dune buggy, Mia thought. Eventually, the road would be smoothed to neat gravel, so shuttles could drive the very young, very old, and whoever didn't feel like walking to the observatory at night. The road meandered gradually past a bend in the river, its chalky green water contrasting with the rust-red rocks it cut through.

Stopping the engine for a minute, Sam pointed down at the swift waters below, "There's a storm coming in the next day or two. These little canyons become giant washes if the rain falls quickly enough. Always know the weather and have an escape plan if you go down into a canyon. You don't want to fall in the wash."

Steep stone walls enclosed the river for as far as Mia could see, layered by time. On this side, a shallow slope led down to the water, almost a rust-red Caribbean beach, but surrounded by vertical walls. She looked down into the canyon and shuddered a little at the sheer cliffs on either side. She wouldn't want to be caught on a flooding river, with those cliffs as the only way out.

By the river's side, there was more vegetation in the bosque, tough bushes and trees that could survive droughts and floods. Their trunks twisted into cracks in impossible rock walls, their contorted shapes stretching for the sun. Rocks piled up like a giant's blocks at the edge of the river. Away from the water, the rust colored desert stretched to the mountains. The only hints of green were the spikes of cacti and dull khaki of scrubby bushes. The air smelled hot and dry, like the inside of a sauna. "It doesn't seem as if it could possibly rain that much here."

"Oh, it does. I didn't believe it either until I saw it," Sam told her. "Flooding is a huge problem here because it doesn't rain very often or very much, usually. Buildings and roads aren't always set up to deal with even a small amount of rain. Parking lots turn into lakes in just a few minutes. Total mess. Then it doesn't happen for a while, and people forget and build something else that floods when it rains." He shook his head at their stupidity. "If only people thought about water flow when they built stuff. I wouldn't build a house in a fifty-year flood zone. Heck, I'd skip the hundred-year one, too. It's not like floods are on an exact schedule."

Mia smiled a little and looked up at the mountains, their bulk blocking the sun's glare. "Is that the observatory?" She pointed to a mountain with a slightly flattened top. Small dots of people could be seen moving around the plateau, hard at work.

"That's it," Sam said cheerfully, revving the engine and careening up the deeply rutted road.

After one spine-shattering jolt, Mia concentrated on holding onto her seat. The little car rocketed past the observatory with a quick wave, climbing into the mountains. They were already very high up.

Sam pointed, the other hand barely on the wheel, to Mia's unvoiced dismay, "You see that road there?"

Mia nodded, "The one to that mountain?"

"That's it!" Sam moved to a lower gear as the road steepened. "It's actually not terrible that we had to move the observatory location. The first place was better for a serious observatory, more sky view since it wasn't as blocked by surrounding mountains. The new location is better for a hotel observatory. Still a good sky view, but a heck of a lot easier for guests to get to." He shook his head, "I don't know how they would have ever built a road to the first site that didn't wash out in

164

storms."

Mia said cheerfully, "Sometimes things are meant to be. Without the construction work, we would never have discovered the flute."

"True," Sam agreed. "But we wouldn't have a murder on our hands either." He shook his head like a dog shaking off water. "You'll have to come back for a sunset ride sometime. There's a fantastic view—you can see the whole valley from there. When everything turns red in the sunset—wow—just wow." Sam looked hesitantly at his aunt. "It's a bit rougher than this road, though. They didn't finish the first road. No point." He slowed a little.

"Can this dune buggy handle it?" she patted the little car.

"A side-by-side, Aunt Mia," he told her, rolling his eyes at her. "Of course it can. This is what it's made for."

"Lead on, Sam," she ordered impatiently. Mia was not going to let a rough road deter her. If Sam had been there before, it should be fine. She hoped.

The side-by-side stirred up choking clouds of red dust as they pulled off Deer Canyon Trail and climbed toward the mountains. "The archaeologists checked out all over this butte and the new construction site for ancestral Pueblo Indian villages," Sam yelled over the engine. "but they didn't find anything much, so they moved on. They finished up a few weeks ago, right after the film crew came." He grinned, "I think they stayed just long enough to do their Indiana Jones bit on film."

"Probably," Mia smiled. "Is it far?"

"No, just around that bend and up the hill. The mountains open into a flat space there."

When Sam said up the hill, he really meant up. The side-by-side climbed higher and higher, slipping on rounded rocks, but steadily making progress up the mountainside. Mia made the mistake of looking out over the path's side once. A foot away from the rugged tires, the path dropped off sharply to the green river, far below. She glanced at Sam, his lips tight in eager concentration as the tires slipped and spun on the rocky path perched hundreds of feet up a cliff. Mia wished she'd chosen to walk up the mountain instead of being strapped in her seat at what felt like a vertical angle. This trail was no place for a vehicle.

A few more minutes of jolting up the steep mountain path, and they arrived at a large flat aerie floating above the surrounding mountains. They were high up in the clear air, but the bulk of the mountains was still in the distance. She could see for miles around, the desert lay out before her like a dusty brown quilt stitched with soft greens.

Mia now understood why the ancient Pueblo people had lived here. Up here, at the feet of the mountains, you would see herds of animals or invading humans for miles around. She breathed in the dusty, thin air, wondering what the history of this little butte was.

This little occupied butte. She turned to Sam, "Is anyone supposed to be camping up here?"

"No, the archaeologists left weeks ago. No one

should be here except hikers or, well, until yesterday, trail riders from the hotel. Not many people come up here since it takes most of the day to do, even on horseback. Most people prefer quicker excursions." He frowned at the clear signs of habitation.

Two small tents and an elaborate canopy shelter stood near the middle of the flat area. A beat-up Land Rover Defender 110, tires splattered with mud, was parked next to the tents. The tents looked like they'd been there a while, from their coating of reddish dust.

Two men moved slowly and carefully around a large pit dug into the sandy ground. As they came closer, Mia recognized the two men she'd seen showering at the pool recently. The older man still had on the same Grateful Dead t-shirt, but his long gray hair was neatly tied back in a long braid. His head barely showed since he was deep in the large hole, newly dug.

The younger man wore a cowboy hat and a long-sleeved sun shirt. Calling out, he jumped out of the pit and waved his arms as they drove up, "Hey, be careful, don't get too close to the excavations. That side-by-side could collapse the whole dig." He glared at the invaders.

"What is going on here?" Mia immediately demanded. "No one's supposed to be camping on the hotel property. And you're digging on the hotel grounds." The recently dug gaping hole was undeniable.

"We're just camping here, not doing anyone any harm," the young man said, clenching his fists.

"We've got every right to be here, same as you."

Sam called back, shutting off the roar of the engine, "She's the hotel owner, and I'm on the team here." He set his jaw a little, clearly wondering if there was going to be an actual fight with the trespassers. He stated firmly, "There's no camping allowed on hotel property."

The other man resounded with belligerence, legs widespread in a fighting stance, "Oh, yeah?"

Mia quickly slid out of the side-by-side, legs slightly wobbly after the jolting ride up here. "Hello, I'm Mia Spinel." She stepped between the two men.

She firmly held out her hand to the younger man, who wiped his hand on his pants before shaking hers truculently. "Nathan." He crammed his hat down on his forehead, glaring out at her pugnaciously. "We've every right to be here."

Ignoring him, Mia nodded affably to the older man, still buried deep as a gopher in his excavation. "Hello."

He nodded wary acknowledgement, "Ed." He stayed, half concealed in his hole, protecting his territory.

"So, what are you all doing here?" she asked in a no-nonsense voice.

"We donated some fossils to the auction the hotel is having, you know, the one funding the museum wing," Nathan said, scuffing his feet in the dust. "We wanted to stick around, go to the opening party to see them auctioned off, and see the exhibit. Maybe pick up something interesting at the auction tonight. It'll be as close as we can get to that flute."

Ed added, "Supposed to be really unique. I want to see it up close." He gradually crept up the sides of his hole, exposing bony dirt-encrusted knees.

"I see," Mia said. "But why are you camping up here, not staying in the hotel?"

"Hotels are way too expensive, just money wasted on fripperies. We'd rather spend money on the actual experience, not just a fancy room. Out here, we can really experience the nature, embrace the past." The older man looked defiantly at her. "Hotels are just stuffy, expensive boxes."

Mia looked at their tents. She'd helped to organize camping excursions from Spinel hotels around the world. She knew enough to tell that the two men had the latest in high-tech equipment. The two tents and rack of foldable solar panels easily cost more than several weeks at the hotel. Their Defender was a serious off-road vehicle. Money was clearly not their primary reason for camping. That left one glaring question.

"Why are you digging here?" Mia kept her voice level.

The large pit in the middle of the flat plain was undeniable. They'd clearly tried their best to keep it safe for anyone who ventured way up here, surrounding it by stringed poles with tiny orange flags. But this butte was hotel property, and they'd dug a pit in it. An actual pit in hotel grounds.

"Oh, this?" Ed gestured casually around the hole his head had barely shown in, as if the hole big enough to hide a platoon wasn't really there. "This was already here when we got here."

"Excuse me?" Mia didn't buy that one.

Nathan added with a rueful smile, "Not exactly, Ed." He smiled ingratiatingly at Mia, tipping back his hat, "I mean, the archaeologists had filled it back in."

"Did a damn lousy job," Ed growled. He patted an edge of the hole, sharpening the precise perpendicular angle.

"Well, yes, they did. Extremely sloppy dig." Nathan turned to Mia. "We thought the university archaeologists had been too hasty in dismissing this site. So with the hole already partially dug for us, we decided to do a proper survey. It seemed unbelievable that an artifact like the flute could be an isolated find."

"I see." Mia wasn't sure how to respond yet.

Sam went over to the edge of the hole, leaning in over the string. His feet clumsily pushed a few rocks into the excavation, and Ed scowled, ducking back into the pit to retrieve them. "This looks deeper than the archaeologists had dug it," Sam commented dubiously.

"Well, yes," Nathan agreed, a cheerful smile broadening his face. "As we thought, they hadn't gone deep enough." He tipped his cowboy hat back proudly.

Mia went over and looked for herself, careful not to disturb the edge. It was a deep pit with very straight sides, connected to other dug-out areas like some massive Tetris game. Each rectangular section was carefully labeled with white number markers. It looked surprisingly professional for two people digging illegally on private property. She wondered why no one had seen their lights at night. "Have you found anything?"

"Yes!" the young man beamed at her. She'd finally asked the right question. "We found the most amazing pottery fragments. Definitely ancestral Pueblo Indian origin."

Ed cut in, "But some have motifs associated with the Woodland Indians. That's a long way away."

"From the Midwest?" Mia questioned. "That is a long way."

"The Woodland culture ranged from the Midwest down to the South, maybe even as far as Georgia," Nathan corrected her enthusiastically. "To find connections between those cultures is something archaeologists dream of. Come see what we've found." He pointed to the long table under the shaded awning, covered in tiny clay shards.

"I'm wondering if this area was a trade route." Ed leaped out of the pit, his gangly legs striding up the red wall like a sidewalk.

There must be hidden steps, Mia thought, as she peered into the straight-sided pit.

He excitedly seized her arm with wiry strength and marched her to the very edge of the high cliff. "Now, look over there. The river was obviously much larger at an earlier point in time. This place would have been perfectly situated to see arriving cargo coming down the river." His eyes gazed fervently across the desert, tracing the possible ancient river paths. "This may have been an ancient trading post, a city, even."

He went on before she could speak, "Woodland Indians had their important chief live on top of a huge mound, a manmade mountain. Maybe the ancestral Pueblo Indians did too. Or perhaps this mountain was a place of worship, and we'll find evidence of their houses on the side of the mountain, like Mesa Verde. Or the plain below."

"Interesting," Mia agreed, politely extricating herself from Ed's sinewy grip and stepping back from the steep edge a little. "Well, as the hotel owner, I normally would ask you to leave. You can't just dig up private property without permission."

Ed waved his arms, "You can't do that. This is science."

Ignoring his protest, Mia continued in a louder tone, "But under the circumstances, you have my permission to excavate here." She looked sternly at them, "However, anything you find goes to the museum."

"If they want it," Nathan said dispiritedly. "They're usually not that interested in pottery shards, which is what we've been finding. They always say they're not attention grabbing enough for a museum audience today."

"That's a shame," Mia said. "I think potteries are my favorite finds. Each tells little stories of people's everyday lives." She spread her hands wide, "Okay, if the museum wants it, they can have it. Or we might set up a permanent exhibit at the hotel if there's anything interesting. And I want to see everything before you move any of it off-site."

"Don't like to keep much on site, so we don't have too much to show you," Ed told her. "Leads to trouble. Not that we've found much so far. Still at the beginning stages, since we didn't get started until after the university team left, of course." He waved his hand at the canvas shaded table. "It's all right there."

"That sounds like a good policy."

"Yeah, especially after all the publicity around that damn flute," Ed said. "I mean, it's good you're donating it, and I guess you want the publicity. That's why most people donate stuff. Or tax breaks," he added sourly.

"The publicity for the hotel is how we can afford to donate it," Mia said tartly. "Remember, we could have just sold it to the highest bidder."

"No one would sell it to a private collector. It's part of human history," he said, eyes wide with shock.

"Sure they would, Ed. Most people would. It's worth a lot of money," Nathan reminded him with a little smile.

"But the value to humanity! Even if they can't touch it or play it, people can see it."

"Well, no one's seeing it now," Sam told them bitterly. "It was stolen last night."

"No!" Nathan cried out, aghast.

"Was that all the noise last night?" Ed asked, curious. "We heard the lights and sirens. Looked like a fire, but it was out by the time we got dressed to go help."

"There was a fire," Sam told him. "They burnt down the stables."

"Oh no," Nathan exclaimed. "The stables? That's what it looked like, but I couldn't see much last night, and we've been working all morning, while it's cooler. It really was the stables. Oh, man." He took off his hat, running his hand through his sweaty dark hair.

"Horses get out?" Ed asked, his deep-set eyes shifting away to the distant horizon.

"The horses are safe, but a man was killed during the robbery at the hotel," Mia told them. "Since we think the only way for the thief to escape was into the hotel or grounds, we wanted to get an idea of where the thief escaped to. No vehicles left the grounds by the main road after the theft; the emergency vehicles saw to that because of the arson. Police have patrolled them ever since."

Sam added, "And this is the only side-by-side allowed out today. Guests are being told everything is out for maintenance."

"And I would guess the horseback trail rides are not available after last night. So the flute is still on the hotel grounds," Nathan said thoughtfully. "Huh." He surveyed the desert below him, as if the flute would magically appear.

"I wondered if you'd seen anything suspicious since you can see the entire hotel grounds from up here. We actually came up to check out the landscape and see if there were any obvious hiding places for a thief or any trails leaving the property. I haven't been at the hotel for very long, so I wanted the bird's eye view." Mia gestured at the vast landscape they could see from their aerie. "Then we found you."

"Well," Ed began, faded brown eyes scanning the landscape, "we missed the early part of the excitement."

"We usually turn in early," Nathan explained. "It's too big a hassle running the generator for lights to work late."

And that explains no one seeing their lights at night, Mia thought.

"And we might miss something on the artifacts or in the excavation without good lighting. So early to bed, early to rise in archeology," said Ed pedantically. He closed his eyes, obviously deep in thought. "Well, we heard the noise, people yelling, and horses going crazy."

"It was pretty bad, those awful screams," Nathan agreed with a grimace. "So I got up, went over to see what the commotion was," he pointed to where the cliff edge overlooked the hotel complex. "We can see everything from here, like you said. But it's pitch dark on a new moon night, except for the fire, so it was hard to see what was going on. Just the lights, really."

Hotel buildings spread out before them like tiny blocks on a model train set.

Nathan commented, "That stable sure is a mess."

Mia noticed people, small as ants, moving purposefully around the black shell of the stable. "It's ruined. It will have to be completely rebuilt." They'd got the horses out, she thought, trying to cheer herself.

"We could see the fire clearly," Nathan continued. "So we got dressed to go help."

"Fire spreads quicker than you think in scrub." Ed nodded to the mountains, "Some of those piñon trees are damned old. Don't want a thousand years gone in minutes."

Nathan continued, "We took another look to plan our route down to the stables, and firetrucks were already there. So we figured we'd be in the way after that."

"Nothing we could do better than firemen with the right equipment," Ed shrugged.

"So we just watched for any sparks showing up for a while, then went back to bed."

"There was one really odd thing," Ed said, jamming his hands in his pockets. "Someone must have been riding last night." He looked disapprovingly at Mia, "That's not safe, you know. Dark hides all kinds of things. Could cripple a horse."

Mia nodded in brisk agreement. "Yes?"

"We saw the rider going down the mountainside. Must have started not too far away from us," he pointed across the hills, "toward the stables. They had a small flashlight. Not traveling fast."

"Too fast for riding in the dark on the mountain," Nathan commented.

"Not safe," Ed agreed. "They got almost to the stables. Then I guess they saw the commotion." He shook his head. "So they just slipped off the poor horse and left it in the desert."

"He was carrying something heavy in his backpack," Nathan said. "It almost overbalanced him when he slid off. No saddlebags. He left the saddle on the horse," he added with disgust.

"Him?" Mia asked.

"He, she, or it, I couldn't see from so far away." He thought a minute. "Not short or very tall, not noticeably fat from this distance. Just an average silhouette with a heavy backpack."

"But they couldn't be the flute thief, Aunt Mia," Sam objected, frowning. "Not if they were on the mountain when the fire started."

"They could be the horse thief," Mia stated. "Which would mean the horse thefts and the murder and theft weren't connected, or at least they were committed by different people."

She thought for a minute. "No, that's not right. They might have started the fire, then gone riding in the mountains. They had to have been at the stable at some point if they rode a horse."

"So the person riding at night is a horse thief?" Ed asked. "We've noticed them a few times." He looked out at the mountains. "Didn't like it, someone riding at night."

Mia nodded, "Someone has been stealing horses at night."

"Huh. We'll keep our eyes out for them, then," Ed told her. "We don't have phone service here, but I can radio in to the sheriff's office if I see anything."

"Good," Mia replied. She looked out over the landscape. Looking out over the layout, she realized there was a more direct path than the road between the hotel and stable, if you were willing to chance not seeing a rattlesnake. Even if the fire had been on a fuse timer of some kind, the thief could have easily made it back to the hotel by the time the first flames were spotted.

She asked, "Were they always coming down the mountain? Or did they take different paths?"

Nathan tipped his sweat-stained hat back. "We noticed the rider a few times, coming from the new observatory area and taking the road down. That's why we thought they were working out a touring route."

"We did wonder. Just one person isn't much of a tour," Ed chuckled.

Nathan commented, "I saw two riders one night. One way behind the other, so far back they might not have been connected. That trail is the best way into the mountains."

"Really?" Mia said. "How long has this been going on?"

"I first saw riders a week or two ago I think, I think." Nathan looked at Ed. "That about right?"

"About that," Ed agreed. "Started about the time those weird explosions happened."

"Explosions?" Mia asked sharply.

"Yeah, maybe work for the observatory?" Nathan suggested.

Sam shook his head. "No, they didn't use explosives for that, either time. Just excavators."

"You know, Neal, the man who is so interested in aliens, mentioned strange lights in the sky. I wonder if it's the same event?" Mia asked.

"No other lights I know of," Ed offered. "No little green men either." He chuckled. "I'd have noticed them." His shoulders lifted. "We've been here a few weeks. Definitely small explosions, but only at night, like you'd use clearing rock on a building site. Nothing too big, so we assumed it was the observatory construction."

"Interesting," Mia said. "I don't know if it has anything to do with the murder, but it's something to consider. And I'd very much like to catch that horse thief."

8

Small Pleasures

Shortly after her dusty desert ride, Mia lay on a table enveloped in soft towels, being pummeled into relaxation by Abby at the hotel spa. "I love the new spa redo, Ms. Mia," Abby was telling her. "The old one, it was so tired. Paint peeling, cabinets broken, all that kind of thing. This new one isn't exactly fancy with crystal chandeliers and everything covered in gold leaf, like when I worked in Las Vegas. It's more just a nice place to be, with all the natural wood and stone, not putting on a show. Somewhere to go when you want to relax and leave feeling and looking better. I love sending people on their way with smiles on their faces."

Her jet-black bob—modernized with wispy ends—swung along with large, brilliantly beaded earrings as she massaged Mia. A tiny silver nose ring decorated one freckled nostril, and her feet were shod in bright pink running shoes. Abby was tiny, with a wiry strength that made nothing of the knots in Mia's shoulders.

The spa was a very nice place to be, Mia agreed.

The warm ochres and soft pinks, combined with soft lighting, enveloped the guests in a soothing atmosphere. All the corners were softly rounded, smoothed adobe surfaces. Handmade tiles lined the floor, the slight variations making the floor interesting but with no jarring notes. The orange blossom aroma from the groves around the hotel was given a subtle spicy note in the spa. Perhaps a hint of cloves and pine? She sleepily wondered what piñon trees smelled like. The faint scent wafting through the rooms uplifted and enhanced the experience. Somewhere, nearby water splashed into a little pool surrounded by ferns, a welcoming sound in the dry desert air.

Discreet speakers played Native American flute music, reminding Mia of the flute. She remembered Ed and Nathan complaining about never hearing the flute play music. She wondered if the simple bone flute could play complicated melodies or if it would just be a few repeated notes. Perhaps a call for worship or a hunting party? Or maybe just a simple child's toy, made precious by age.

With a slight qualm, Mia realized Abby was still talking about the new spa. "You wouldn't believe all the people who come through here in a day, Ms. Mia." Her jet-black hair swung in a silken sheet as she worked. "We get all kinds. That woman, Destiny, you know, the one who haunts the spirit room, she always comes in at the last minute, demanding an appointment right then." She shook her head in disgust. "Like she's," Abby drew out the word, "the most important person who comes in here."

Recalling Destiny's muddy boots and unkempt clothes, Mia felt a slight pang of guilt over her impromptu appointment. That jarred with the spa's intensely feminine atmosphere. "She doesn't seem the type of person who would use the spa facility. One would think she'd do more outdoor activities."

"That's usually true. I know she's always at the hotel because she leaves some stories in her wake, I can tell you, but she rarely comes in here. Just her nails occasionally. Thank goodness," Abby exhaled the phrase with a sigh. "Her hands were absolutely destroyed this morning. Looked like she'd been doing heavy gardening without gloves. Scratched and torn everywhere."

"I wonder why?"

"She says," Abby emphasized the word with a turn of her head that set her beaded earrings dancing, "she says she slipped and fell while hiking."

"And you don't believe her?" Mia asked curiously.

"It's possible," Abby said doubtfully. "People do slip and fall, get their hands torn up. Just the way she said it seemed off. I wondered if she fell somewhere she wasn't supposed to be. It wouldn't surprise me if she snooped around the hotel."

"Somewhere like the new observatory site?" Mia suggested.

The earrings swung, bright colors dancing against the dark bob. "Interesting. No guests are supposed to be at the construction site, are they?" She nodded once. "That makes sense. Or maybe digging around the old site, now that the archaeologists have left. Anyway, I fixed her up, gave her a nice manicure, and some aloe salve for the cuts. Atsa's aunt makes the most amazing green goo that fixes everything."

"I'll have to get some," Mia said thoughtfully. "Anyone else interesting this morning?"

"Hmmm," Abby mused. "Estela Wallace? She said you sent her. Now that woman is pure glamour. Reminds me of an old black and white movie star. Not that she's not always in bright colors, but so glamorous."

"She is, isn't she? I love seeing women who know what makes them look good, and she is an expert," Mia agreed. "What did she have done?"

"Oh, a massage, like you're having." Abby laughed. "Pretty big tension knots, just like yours."

Mia moved her shoulders ruefully. "I'm not surprised."

"She had her nails done, too. She gets them touched up every few days. Likes them absolutely perfect," Abby said knowingly. "When you do a lot of riding, your hands show it quickly if you're not careful."

"Estela does that much riding?" Mia was surprised. "I understood she had ridden some and knew Becky, but I didn't know she went that often."

"Oh yes, she's usually out every morning," Abby told her with a smile. "She looks perfect on a horse, too. Total movie star," she sighed. "Some people have all the luck." She shrugged, shaking off the brief moment of envy. "Now, Kyle Lee came in here almost every day." She smiled. "He said he wanted to look perfect for the camera, but I'd guess his mirror was just as important. Still, it's too bad about his death. Really weird that he was there in the middle of the night. He always went on and on about needing his beauty sleep."

"Interesting," Mia encouraged.

"Now, his hands were always perfect. Soft, like he never did anything with them. You can tell a lot about a person from their hands." Abby said, "I like men that do things, you know? What good is a man who can't build stuff?"

"Mmm," Mia said noncommittally. There were many ways for a man to build. "So Kyle was not the building things sort of man."

"Never worked a day in his life, I'd guess," said Abby, massaging Mia's leg with her strong hands.

"That seems odd. I would have thought an archaeologist would have to dig and haul things, at least. No one who does that has perfect hands."

"My guess is he was just the TV version," Abby said dismissively. "Even his hair had to be trimmed every few days, so it was always exactly the same. Like people would notice or care on a documentary." She added, "Emily, the production assistant, came in with her back hurting badly this morning. She said she'd carried all that heavy gear out by herself."

"Yes, I don't think the others on the set helped her much."

"I gave her a deep tissue massage, but told her, in my opinion, she needed a chiropractor. There's a really good one who comes here by appointment, but she said she'd go when she got back home." Abby helped Mia up off the table with a practiced hand. "Anyway, she felt a lot better when she left."

"I'm sure she did," Mia replied. "I know I do."

"You don't want to be barreling around in a side-by-side at your age," Abby ordered her. "Relax by the pool." She grinned, "Pretend you're on vacation for a day or two, like everyone else."

Mia tentatively moved her shoulders in a fluid motion. "Thanks for the massage, Abby. I feel much better."

"Any time," Abby said with a smile.

Feeling at ease after the restful session, Mia paused briefly in the spa's lobby to look at the small koi pond and waterfall. The receptionist asked with a cheerful smile, "Is there anything else you'd like done today, Ms. Mia? Anything you want, we can do."

The receptionist's dewy skin showed not a trace of makeup except the requisite lip stain. She didn't need any.

"I'm curious, Cindy," Mia read her name tag on her neat rose pink uniform. "What are your most popular treatments?" She loved finding new spa treatments. "What do you like?" The hospitality team always had the opportunity to try a few hotel services every month, so they could tell guests about them.

"Well, the full body massage is always a classic," the young woman said. "People get stressed, want to unwind, you know?" She thought a minute. "Basic stuff like nails, hair. The stylist here is fabulous." She smoothed her brown hair, just touched with highlights. "I go whenever I get the chance."

"They did a lovely job, Cindy," Mia said sincerely. "The hints of gold are perfect."

"I know, right? Paul is a freaking genius with hair. I've been trying to get Emily, you know, with the production company, to go. She can't like looking like a brown mouse that ran through a haystack. But she won't do it. Says she doesn't have time. Why are they making her work after the wrap-up, anyway? Talk about an awful job." Cindy continued, "I do a desert clay facial sometimes." She stroked her face. "It makes my face unbelievably soft, and I don't have any breakouts anymore. And the cactus wrap, of course."

"Cactus wrap?" Mia was startled.

"Without the spines, of course!" Cindy laughed gaily as she ushered Mia out.

A few minutes later, a completely pampered Mia sipped perfectly chilled champagne from the balcony perched above the lobby. She leaned against the high-backed carved chair and surveyed the scene below. The steady flow of people was reassuring for a hotel owner, especially one who had just had a murder in their hotel. People stood in line three deep at the concierge's desk, most leaving with a cheerful smile or a handful of tickets, planning their next adventure this trip. No piles of luggage leaving, just the normal ebb and flow of a hotel lobby. Kyle's murder may not be forgotten, but it wasn't disrupting her guests' vacations. Good.

With a flourish, Sam appeared with a tray of hor d'oeuvres, "Milady." Miniature tortillas adorned a carved wood tray. "Chef Chooli thought the guests would like some snacks. Just getting the party started," he said with a grin.

"Very good idea," Mia agreed. "Always feed guests during unexpected times—and every other occasion." She took a tiny plate and perused the selection. "What do you suggest?"

"The adobe sauce ones are delicious," he pointed. "And the smoked fish I could eat by the handful."

"Thanks, Sam." The little nibbles were perfect, just the right prelude to dinner. She slowly sipped her champagne and walked down the cool, dark hall to the terrace. People were already grouping around the pool for the upcoming party. From the laughter drifting past, Susan had done a good job putting out the word.

She surveyed the gentle slopes around the hotel, leading up to the steep mountains. Now that Mia knew the landmarks, she could see tiny clouds of dust around the new observatory site as construction trucks left for the day. Further up the mountain, the high perch where the flute had been found commanded a view of the entire area. The evening view from there must be spectacular.

Why would someone steal horses at night and ride into the mountains? While teenagers, and some old enough to know better, might steal a horse once for an equine joy ride, repeated occurrences spoke to a purpose behind the thefts. Committing a felony, not once but multiple times, meant there was a reason someone needed to ride that horse—something they couldn't do on a regular trail ride.

188

Strange lights, possible explosions, and mysterious visitors had sprung into gossip about the same time the horse thefts started. While Mia was open to the possibility of aliens, she simply didn't believe in that possible explanation under these circumstances, no matter how enthusiastic Neal Mjesec was. Surely aliens capable of traveling through light-years of space and landing on Earth would have no need to borrow a horse.

Someone was up to something nefarious in those mountains, not far out of sight from the hotel. Either they were removing something hidden in the rocks, or they were hiding something in those same rocks. From what she could see, it would be easy to find a crevice or cave no one had explored for a thousand years in the foothills. What a perfect place to hide loot from a robbery, she thought. The thief could return at their leisure, secure in the knowledge no one would find their treasure in the vast landscape. But why had they started the trips before the robbery occurred? Surely one exploratory trip at night would be enough to find a suitable crevice, and it could be checked during a trail ride, quite casually during the day.

Savoring the crisp champagne, Mia leaned on the railing. The first streaks of orange crept into the sky, decorating the hotel complex in golden light. She was starting to understand how the robbery had been done, but so much turned on what kind of man Kyle had been.

She stepped back into the hotel through the large French doors, appreciating the cool tiles beneath her neat velvet heels. The tiles looked ancient and had certainly been here longer than recent renovations. Handmade tiles were still available, but with nothing like the subtle charm and variations beneath her. Most were mere crude imitations that screamed handmade. She noted that the large doors to the terrace were obviously a later addition, despite their ornately carved trim.

The main hotel building was much older than she had initially assumed when she arrived. So many layers of renovations had been done, most in keeping with the original building, like those lovely doors, but some far removed, like the sterile hospitality team hall.

Once, this must have been a grand ranch indeed, she thought as she looked at the intricately carved stairway and massive lobby. Huge ceiling beams stretched across the large span, obviously worn by time. Blackened streaks like alligator skin marred several beams. There must have been a fire at some point, but enough of the structure had lasted to make it worthwhile to repair the ranch from the ruins, unlike the stable.

A hundred or more years ago, an isolated prosperous ranch would have attracted thieves and marauders. From the Spanish in what was now Mexico to wandering Western outlaws, a large ranch would have been a rich target. The main building would have been built for protection, not just from the sun, but from invaders, like an ancient castle. The thick walls surrounding her and the heavy wood shutters standing guard to small windows told her that story. Large windows were later additions, a testament to the safer world they lived in—and insulated glass keeping out the summer heat.

How long had the original family and their wealth survived? They must have been cattle ranchers, sending cattle back to the East or the newfound wealth of the West Coast. Why else would they have lived out here, so far from civilization?

Mia ran her hand along the smooth, carved wood and wondered how the long-ago ranchers had flourished enough to have carved panels and intricate balconies.

She settled back in her chair overlooking the lobby, watching the evening scene unfold below her like a play. The earliest diners were arriving, hungry after their day's adventures. The crowd was smaller than normal, many diners opting for the poolside buffet. The dress code at this casual resort was relaxed, but Mia noticed Tahoma frowning slightly at a large, argumentative man in a loud Hawaiian shirt. She smiled a little at Tahoma's reaction. The man was unlikely to be seated in a prime location. Headwaiters were proud of their restaurants and expected appropriate respect from their guests.

She was a little surprised to see Ed and Nathan, the two archaeologists, arrive spiffed up for dinner. She hoped they hadn't used the pool shower again, but supposed it was better than no shower. She was surprised they hadn't stayed poolside for the free buffet.

They looked quite distinguished compared to

earlier, in well-fitted sports coats over button-down shirts. Ed's hair was neatly combed into a silvery braid, and Nathan had abandoned his Indiana Jones hat. Looking around the lobby, they nodded in approval while pointing to the old beams and adobe fireplace, clearly appreciating things that weren't over a thousand years old. Mia found it amusing that they didn't have a problem eating at the world-class restaurant. They just didn't want to pay to stay at the hotel. People were odd about what they would spend money on—and what they wouldn't.

She wondered if the two men had any connection to the theft and Kyle's murder. Just because they claimed to have seen a rider didn't mean they weren't the actual horse thieves. A horse would be very useful for scouting out possible clandestine dig sites. The archaeologists seemed to genuinely care about the artifacts and their role in history, but they also didn't have a lot of respect for most scholars. No wonder, if the university archaeologists had sloppily left so many discoveries in the ground. She wouldn't be surprised if the pair followed official digs around, collecting remnants.

Estela entered the lobby, her graceful curving figure commanding the center of attention, as always. The Wallaces made a beeline over to the archaeologists, smiling and waving. Nathan embraced Estela with gusto, shaking John's hand at the same time. Obviously, they knew each other well and were meeting for dinner. That would explain the archaeologists' respectable clothing.

Perhaps Ed and Nathan had worked on Estela's father's or one of John's digs. Mia knew John made archeological and paleontological discoveries on his own land from time to time. Knowing John and his views on museum collections, she wouldn't be surprised if he brought in his own team to excavate.

"Penny for your thoughts," a voice boomed, almost in her ear.

Mia jumped a little, "Pete, you startled me! I think I was a million miles away."

"Worrying about Kyle's murder?" the cameraman asked with a worried expression.

"Actually, I noticed the old fire damage on the joists there." She pointed. "I was wondering how old the building and ranch actually were."

"Pretty old, I'd guess," he waved someone over. "Here, Emily will know. She's from around here and knows everything about the area."

Emily smiled in greeting, "Emily will know what?" she asked, perching on a chair.

"How old this place is. Ms. Spinel was just asking."

"Wondering about the warranties?" Emily said with a sly laugh. "I think you're a little late." She smoothed back her dull brown hair, fiddling with a diamond stud earring, then straightened her curving shoulders slightly. "Well, let's see. Cattle were kept in this valley since way back when the Spanish missionaries infested the area. Because the river was here, they had a constant water source, absolutely critical in a desert. So the ranch started with a lot of cattle and a few seasonal shacks in the 1700's. The original owner, Jack Addison, bought all the land in the valley about 1840 and built this house." Emily smiled a little, "There are all kinds of rumors that Addison was a wanted man back East, escaping criminal charges, like murder and arson. I couldn't get a good source confirming anything, so I wondered if he changed his name or paid someone off." She shrugged.

"I would have back then," Pete commented, fiddling with his ponytail. "All a wanted man had to do was travel, and no one would know who they were."

"So Addison arrives here and builds the grandest house in the neighborhood, supposedly to lure a local girl to marry him, but even the house wasn't enough for her to choose him." Emily smoothed her gray skirt a little. "Stories abound of wild parties and attacks by bandits. Some even said Jack Addison was the outlaw ringleader for a bunch of stagecoach robberies. The Pinkertons came to town investigating the robberies, and the sheriff even searched his house. That was in the local paper, but they never found anything. Addison's reputation was completely ruined after the accusations, not that it was great before them. Finally, Jack Addison kidnapped the girl. Back then, she had to marry him after that."

"Very different times," Mia said with distaste.

"They were," Emily agreed, rolling her eyes. "Of course, some bad relationships are almost impossible to get out of, even now." She tucked her hair behind her ear and twisted her earring. Little sparks of light from the diamond made a bright kaleidoscope on her gray sweater. "So around then, the California Gold Rush starts and money starts rolling in from cattle sales. Addison expanded the ranch even more, adding onto both land and buildings until it was the largest in northern Arizona. When the California gold rush ended, he lucked out and found gold on his own land."

"On this property?" Mia asked curiously.

"Somewhere on the ranch. I don't think it was a huge amount, just enough to fuel even further ranch expansion. The real wealth was in cattle. Apparently, the last owners tried to develop the old mine. They must not have found much, or they wouldn't have gone bankrupt."

Glancing down at the lobby, Mia saw Neal Mjesec hurrying past the well-dressed people waiting for the restaurant. His shoes and pants were coated in red dust, as if he'd been collecting his samples in the desert. He carried an aluminum case furtively, as if someone might try to take it away. She smiled at his enthusiasm.

Emily said, "Jack Addison really led a charmed life for someone with such a bad reputation. There was all kinds of talk about it. There are a lot of stories around, even now."

"There always are," Mia said.

"Some even said he was in league with the devil, and that's why everything he did prospered."

"Sounds like jealousy," Pete commented.

"Or he was crooked. Lots of luck is made, both honestly and dishonestly," Mia said.

"Either way, he lived to a ripe old age and left

the ranch to his oldest son, Jack Jr. His wife died twenty years before that, even though she was so much younger. They said she wasn't allowed to leave the ranch, just stayed locked up in her room."

"Probably scared she would run away. Wonder if he killed her," Pete commented.

"I think it was probably the gazillion children she had," Emily told him. "No one but Jack Jr inherited. Some stayed, and all seemed to get along. The history gets a lot more boring after that."

"Probably nicer for those living it," Mia said.

"Probably," Emily agreed. "The last Addison died about thirty years ago, and donated the ranch to the local children's charity, who didn't want the property. They sold it to people who ran a spiritual retreat. And that's when it became a hotel."

"My goodness," Mia exclaimed. "You do know this place. Pete said you grew up around here?"

"Not too far away, but really, I researched the ranch for the documentary. You never know when something interesting will pop up. And Destiny helped a lot, too." She pointed down into the lobby. To her surprise, Mia saw Destiny, dressed in an unfortunate floaty chiffon gown clinging to all the curves she didn't want, going into dinner with the Wallaces, Ed and Nathan. She wondered what they could have in common.

Emily continued enthusiastically, "She was an absolute gold mine of knowledge about this ranch." She shrugged and gave a laugh, "I think Destiny is a bit cracked on the subject, to tell the truth. Once she

196

started telling me the history, it was hard to get her to stop."

"I can imagine," Mia said with a smile.

"That woman who yammers on about her spirit room?" Pete asked.

"That's the one," Emily agreed. "She gave me the complete tour once and started howling like a wolf." She shivered a little, drawing her light grey sweater tighter. "The echoes in there were incredibly creepy, bouncing endlessly off the walls."

"Sounds like the spirits spooked you," Pete joked.

Laughing at herself, Emily shifted her feet. "All I know is if we ever do a documentary on haunted houses, that's the effect I'm going for."

"I'm afraid that particular room will no longer be available, Mia told them. "I don't think this hotel needs a spirit room."

"Well, I can't blame you," Pete said. "Hotel guests probably don't go in for the voodoo stuff."

"Oh, I don't know," Emily said. "Spookiness in one room probably isn't bad. I stayed at a hotel in England that charged extra for their haunted rooms."

"I wouldn't sleep in a haunted room," Pete returned. "I mean, I don't believe in ghosts, but still."

"Me either," Emily agreed. "But a haunted room in a hotel, where it's confined to one place you're not sleeping, that's pretty fun."

"And not something every hotel has. Interesting," Mia said. "I will have to look into that once I have our other problem fixed. I haven't even been in the spirit room."

"I've heard it." Pete sipped his Scotch slowly. "Spirits sure are loud."

"The other problem?" Emily questioned with a frown. "Is that Kyle's murder?"

"And recovering the stolen objects. Yes," Mia smiled at them. "You've given me a lot to think about. I think we should tell the hotel's history in a brochure or a little exhibit." She stood up, "Now, would you two lovely people like to join me for dinner?"

"Absolutely," Pete agreed.

"Well, I probably should get back to work," Emily said, shuffling her feet, looking for a graceful way out.

"Don't be silly, Emily. You have to eat," Mia ordered.

"Well, thank you, then," Emily accepted awkwardly, shrugging her slumped shoulders.

Tahoma whisked them to a quiet alcove, seating Mia so she commanded a view of the room. He filled her glass with the golden bubbles of her favorite champagne and gave them the specials, with an intriguing addition of venison in wild plum sauce, which she promptly ordered.

The important business of selecting their meals completed, they settled back in their chairs. The sound of soft classical guitar filled the room.

"The original inhabitants of this ranch would have had music not too far off this," Emily said, her smile dreamy. "Guitars were invented by the Spanish in the 1600's. Many made it to aboard ships, to while away the long hours. Playing around campfires or in ranch houses at night would have been a favorite entertainment."

"That's the Sonata in D Major, by Mateo Albéniz. One of my favorites," Mia said. "Sam must be playing it for me."

"Play it again, Sam?" Pete joked. "That's some service the boss gets."

Mia smiled. "Sam is my nephew. He must have heard this a hundred times when he came over as a child." She nodded thanks to Sam, and he winked broadly. "It's probably ingrained in his memory permanently, whether he likes it or not."

They laughed as Tahoma arrived with appetizers, a classic platter of local goat cheeses, figs, and honey with tiny crisp flatbreads. They happily chose their favorite combinations to try.

Mia continued, "Sam is working here for a year while he's deciding what training he wants."

"I've seen him bussing tables," Pete commented. "I guess he's learning from the ground up, huh?"

Mia nodded. "He is, indeed." She thoughtfully took a bite of her appetizer. "With all the local food served here, everything must be very similar to what people did way back in the nineteenth century." She nodded to the roaring fire in the fireplace and the candlelit tables. "Firelight makes for a cozy evening now, but things were a little different back then."

"There weren't many trees in the desert," Emily commented. "They would have had to haul in wood from the forests, a little to the north of here."

"Grassland was better for cattle." Mia nodded. "What I've been wondering is how an isolated ranch managed to survive out here, miles from town."

"We have it easy in comparison," Pete agreed. "And when we get tired of carrying logs for a roaring fire, there's always central heating."

"Amen to that," Emily agreed, laughing. They mockingly clinked glasses as their meal arrived.

After all had enjoyed their first bites, Mia asked quietly, "Have you had any problems about Kyle's death? With the police?"

Pete smiled and shrugged. "No big deal. Just what I was doing that night, that sort of thing." He wiggled his shoulders uncomfortably. "I didn't have an alibi, worse luck."

Emily looked a little startled that Mia had brought up Kyle's murder. She made a slight face. "About the same, I guess. I mean, I was asleep. It had been a really hard day. But I don't have any way to prove it."

"They questioned me quite a lot, as well," Mia commiserated. "And I barely knew Kyle." She looked at them. "You both worked with him for a long time. What sort of man was he?"

Pete smoothed his stringy ponytail. "Well, I already told you, I think he was a crook. And his being there, that night, proves it."

"How does that prove anything?" Emily shot back. "Just because he was there doesn't mean he was a thief. He might have seen something, gone to

200

investigate, and been killed."

Pete threw his hands up in the air, saying with exasperation,."Emily, just because you used to date the guy doesn't make him perfect."

Mia broke in, "You used to date Kyle? Oh, Emily, you must be feeling awful about his death."

Emily shook her head emphatically. "We were over a long time ago."

Mia said with sympathy, "Even after a long time, it still makes an unexpected death more difficult if you once cared about him." She patted Emily's hand, and Emily froze like a startled cat, unsure how to deal with sympathy from an almost stranger. Mia quickly removed her hand. "Even if Kyle changed into someone you couldn't date, he must have been a lot of fun to be with, once."

Emily twisted her mouth up. "Once? Yeah, he was a lot of fun to be with, as long as I didn't expect anything too much from him, like showing up on time, or at all." She looked off into distant memory, "Yeah, he was fun. He used to take me behind the scenes on his shows and introduce me around. That's how I got this job, you know. I organized stuff a lot when they needed something. I was always broke because Kyle wasn't exactly responsible about money." She laughed shortly. "Hal told me, let's make the job you're already doing official, so I became his assistant. I stayed on after Kyle, and I broke up. I like the job. The pay is good, and I get to travel everywhere, see all kinds of things, and be paid to do it." She fiddled with her earring.

"You seem to do it very well," Mia praised.

"Yeah, I worked for a museum after I graduated. That's how I met Kyle."

"Really? What museum? What did you do?" Mia asked with polite curiosity.

"I was a researcher for the New Haven Art Museum. I'd look up stuff for special exhibits. Improve the permanent exhibits." Emily's eyes brightened. "Just walking through an exhibit, no matter how amazing it is, gets a little dull for most people after the first room or two." She spread her hands wide, leaning forward as she gesticulated, "But if you show people the stories behind those objects, all of a sudden the past comes alive, and people are interested."

Mia smiled at Emily's enthusiasm. "Really, you're doing the exact same job now, making the past come alive for people. You just have a bigger audience."

Emily smiled back, gratified, "That's true. It's a lot of fun to find out all the stories about a find. Then put it together in a program." She pursed her lips, "The only part I don't like are the actual shoots."

"That's where I come in," grinned Pete. "And that's where Kyle turned into a real jerk."

"He did," Emily agreed, with a sad nod. "It was not his best time."

"Why do you think Kyle got into doing shows in the first place?" Mia asked. "He could have been a working archaeologist with a museum or university."

Emily laughed and spread her hands wide. "Museums don't pay much, and Kyle liked money."

"A lot," Pete confirmed with a grin. "Ran through his fingers like water, but he did like it."

"It was also the chance for him to have a bigger audience," Emily mused. "At a museum, hardly anyone would know he was there. Attention is saved for very few people, and he didn't have the kind of museum donor family that would make rising to a museum director position easy."

"Still, people can do that," Mia said.

Emily shook her head with a smile. "Some people can. People who don't mind hard work. Kyle usually convinced someone else to do anything he thought was boring or difficult." She laughed softly. "No, a museum was not the best place for Kyle, and he knew it."

"What about a university?" Mia suggested. "I know it's publish or perish, but Kyle did publish."

Emily agreed, "He did publish, but not to academic standards. He didn't always cite his sources." Her brow wrinkled. "To tell you the truth, I'm not so sure he didn't make up some of his sources. Sometimes his historical descriptions seemed more like imagination, less like research."

"Could he really get away with that?" Mia asked.

Pete laughed. "Course he could. Kyle could smooth-talk his way out of anything."

Emily explained, "When I asked, he'd always tell me he would love to bring me the book or papers he got it from, he'd look it up and give it to me the next time he saw me. And, of course, he always forgot." She chuckled. "It was hard to know what was real and what was fake, with Kyle."

"I always wondered how he could focus long enough to write the books in the first place. He always got other people to do his stuff for him. Why not the books?" Pete said.

"He was pretty vague on them," Emily agreed. "Do you think he hired a ghostwriter?"

"Wouldn't surprise me," Pete said, draining his whisky. "Well, Mia, thank you for a great dinner. I really enjoyed it." He stood up, and they all rose.

"Thank you, Mia," Emily echoed.

Mia smiled at them both. "I'm glad you could come tonight. Dinner is a meal best shared."

As she walked out into the lobby, Mia noticed Atsa trying to discreetly wave her down.

"What's wrong, Atsa?"

"I found Destiny coming out of the spirit room, Ms. Mia. I thought you'd want to know." Atsa's voice was worried.

"Yes, of course," Mia said. "How ever did she get in there? I thought the door was locked?"

"I thought it was too," Atsa agreed. "But I caught her slipping out of there a few minutes ago, looking like she'd been on a muddy hike, as usual." She tapped her pen on the desk. "She told me she found the door unlocked, and just went in to commune with the spirits," Atsa's tone was lightly mocking, "but I'm sure I locked the door."

"Maybe the cleaners unlocked it? They wouldn't necessarily lock a public room door," Mia suggested.

"I told them not to clean it since it would be

renovated," Atsa said. "We're short-staffed as it is, so I thought one less thing to do." She shrugged, "I guess one could have forgotten. Or security went to check or something."

"Or maybe two hospitality team members took advantage of an empty room to, um, have some alone time," Mia said with a smile. "Well, it doesn't really matter since Destiny didn't disturb the other guests. She couldn't have been there long, since I saw her going in for dinner earlier."

"I just thought you'd like to know since it seemed odd," Atsa told her.

"Thank you," Mia said appreciatively. "With the murder and theft, I want to know about anything that seems odd." She looked around at the quiet lobby. "Has the desk been busy today?"

"It was," Atsa said. "Things have quieted down now. Everyone has had dinner, and they're off to their late evening activity or bed. The pool party was a huge success." She yawned a little, covering her mouth discreetly. "I only have a few more minutes on duty."

"Go home and get a good night's sleep," Mia advised. "Don't let your boss drag you out all night."

Atsa turned her yawn into a laugh. "I won't. Home for me, tonight."

"Good," Mia said. "I'm turning in myself."

9

Digging Deep

The next morning, Sheriff Hank leaned morosely on the railing, looking at the horses. They were running around, playing in the grass, tossing their heads up, and neighing in pleasure on this fine day. "You dumb animals have it lucky," Hank told them. "No one expects you to talk back." He was here on business, accompanying the fire inspector—the most persnickety long drip of tallow he'd ever seen.

The inspector shuffled around the ashes, muttering in a monotone while his assistant dutifully took notes. Technically, Hank had to be at the crime scene, and he knew his duty—especially when there was a killer running loose. However, he didn't have to be next to a durn fool stirring up a cloud of ashes as big as an elephant. If the fire inspector kept messing around, it'd look like a haboob coming.

They'd finally found the horse, Lightning. He'd run almost to a neighboring state to get away from the smoke and fear. Thank the Lord, a rancher called it in last night. Hank hooked up his trailer, fetched the fool horse himself, and sent Rebecca a blurry photo, so she'd quit fussing. She'd been nearly frantic to get that horse. Hank had been worried she'd hurt herself trying to search for him.

Hank scowled at the magnificent horse, shining in the morning sun. "You'd think a horse like you would have better sense," he told Lightning. "You ain't getting a better boss than Miz Rebecca."

The horse snorted and threw up his head, seeming to agree. A startled cry of pain came from behind him. The sheriff whipped around, starting for the ruined barn. "You okay?" he called.

A quaver of a voice came out of the ash cloud. "I'm fine, fine. I trod on a nail. A minor mishap."

"You want to wear better shoes for this kind of work, Mr. Graves," Sheriff Hank replied. "That's a real good way to catch tetanus."

"I will take that into consideration next time, Sheriff," the thin voice replied. "I was told this was a site with minimal detritus."

"Huh," Hank grunted a reply, thinking minimal detritus, my sainted aunt. Didn't the fool know burned buildings always meant nails? Himself, he kept desert hiking snake boots in his truck, just in case. But it wasn't his problem.

He stared at the white horse, thinking about

Rebecca. Coming so close to losing her had scared him badly. He knew it was time to ask her to share their lives together, but he just couldn't do it while she was sick. She was a durn proud woman and wouldn't put up with him fussing over her. That sure made it hard to take care of her.

Rebecca's head injury had proven to be a little more severe than the docs had first thought, but she was healing up well. She was a strong woman and would be fine after some rest. The problem was, she wasn't ready to be on her own, but she hadn't any family left to help her. So Hank had taken to dropping by three or more times a day to check on her. She was doing fine, just needed a little help right now. But the durn hospitals thought about nothing but insurance money. And there was no way Rebecca would step foot in a nursing home under her own steam unless it was to bring someone else a basket of treats on their stint.

"Why didn't you kick the thieves, Lightning?" he muttered. "Then I'd know who hurt Rebecca." The stitches would be a clue. He hadn't got another clue worth speaking of.

The horse snorted. Hank straightened up, tipping his hat against the glare of the sun. Waves of dry winter grass rippled gold in the morning light against the backdrop of purple mountains. Sure was beautiful this morning.

Behind him, he heard a sudden whomp followed by the assistant calling in panic, "Mr. Graves, Mr. Graves."

Ash billowed in the air as he ran toward the

voice. "What happened?"

The assistant squeaked, "I don't know, Sheriff. One minute he was here; the next he was gone. He just disappeared." He dropped his notebook on the ashes and wrung his hands together. "My Gram always said this place was cursed. He disappeared. Vanished into thin air." His feet shuffled on the ashes, and the sheriff sneezed, waiting for the rather thick air to clear. "It's cursed, I tell you!" He backed away, keeping his wary eye on the ruined structure.

A faint, muffled voice emerged from the ash cloud, "I'm here, you fool."

"Where?" the assistant asked, in confusion. The air was starting to clear, but no fire inspector could be seen. He looked around wildly at the blackened timbers and took another step back.

"I'm in a hole," Mr. Graves said, pain obvious in his voice. "Down here." Dust was settling, but it was still impossible to see much.

"What hole?" the assistant repeated, still in slow retreat. "Do you mean the ground just opened up and swallowed you, from the curse?" He clasped his hands together so tightly that white knuckles showed.

Sheriff Hank moved forward cautiously, checking each step for solid ground. "He's in this hole," he pointed down at the ashen face of Mr. Graves, looking up at him. "It looks like there's an old basement underneath the stable."

"There's not supposed to be a basement in the stable," Mr. Graves complained querulously. "There's no basement on the building plans filed with the county.

This stable doesn't have a basement." He peered up at the sheriff.

"Huh," Hank replied, looking at the deep, obviously manmade pit that had lurked under the stable. "Well, I don't think the ground just opened up and laid bricks." He nodded to the fire inspector. "So, how do you want to get out of there? Are you up for a ladder?"

As the dust slowly settled, Hank could see Mr. Graves lying against the wall with his leg twisted at an impossible angle underneath him. Clearly, a ladder was not an option.

Mr. Graves' long, narrow face was drawn with pain. "I believe I will need some slight assistance getting out." He nodded his head at his clearly unreachable pocket. "I don't believe I can make a call myself at the moment. If you would be so kind as to call an ambulance, that would be most thoughtful." His eyes rolled up slightly in his head, and he closed them, as if keeping them open was too much of an effort.

Hank made that call and found a ladder in record time. The fire inspector had passed out, most likely from pain and shock, so Hank kept one finger on his pulse, crouching down in the charcoal next to him. That leg was badly broken; no wonder the pain had been too much for the man.

His eyes wandered around the room, for it was a room. There might not be a basement on the stable plans, but it sure looked like someone had built one. Burnt debris had fallen in along with Mr. Graves, but the fire hadn't reached down here.

It didn't look as if anyone had been here in a long time. A few oil lanterns hung on the wall, where they might come in handy. A stack of rope coils, half-rotted from age. An old wooden table and some chairs with a pack of cards thrown down. Shovels and a pickax were stacked up on the dirt floor. Three walls were dirt, but the fourth was old bricks with a wooden door. Dust lay thick on everything, from the table to the ropes.

But no dust lay on the shiny new flashlight sitting on the table. And the red plastic handle on one shovel betrayed its age. Someone had been down here much more recently than a hundred years ago. He guessed someone had been here this week.

His fingers felt the steady throb of Mr. Graves' pulse, and he itched to find out what was behind the door, hidden down here for so long.

A brief shower of ashes fell on his shoulder, and a shadow blocked the light. "Hello there!" a voice called. "Anything we can do?"

"We were driving to the hotel and saw the ash cloud go up," a second voice confirmed. A head poked into view, neatly braided hair and a Grateful Dead t-shirt confirming Hank's suspicions. "Looks like a hidden room under here," Ed said enthusiastically, already headed down the ladder. "What's behind that door?"

"I don't know yet," Hank told him flatly. "First priority is to get Mr. Graves out of here, then I'll," he emphasized the singular word, "investigate."

Ed's eyes roved the walls in search of artifacts, barely straying to the obviously recent prone body of

Mr. Graves. "Of course, of course."

Nathan clambered down the ladder and whistled. "This is something, isn't it? Looks like it's been here quite a while."

Ed inched closer. "Whatever's behind that door isn't under the stable, is it? Wrong direction."

"Nope," Sheriff Hank told him. "And folks, this is a crime scene, you can't be here."

"Nonsense," Ed told him. "We're used to investigating buried rooms. We can help you." He clearly had no intention of moving, except by force. "I bet something interesting is behind this door." He examined it minutely. "New screws put on the hinges, and the wood's been repaired here." He pointed to fresh timber. "Someone's used it recently."

To Hank's relief, an ambulance raced up with lights and sirens flashing. With some struggle, they got Mr. Graves on a gurney and out of the hole. Unfortunately, the injured man woke briefly during the procedure, but passed out after a petulant, "Quit bouncing me around, you morons."

The sirens brought onlookers, curious about new trouble at the stable. Hank called up, "Get back from the edge, people! Do you want to fall in too?" Motioning to his deputies to cut off access to the area, he saw Sam peering over the edge and called up, "Go tell Miz Mia I need to see her. Right now," he emphasized. Sam's face disappeared in a flash.

Mia cautiously put one pink sneaker on the ladder and bounced it slightly to test it. It didn't budge, so she carefully made her way down, looking around with curiosity once she reached the dirt floor.

"Did you know there was a room here?" Sheriff Hank asked. "The fire inspector said there wasn't a basement on the plans."

"I've seen the stable plans, and there's no indication of a lower floor, not even a storage room or a stairway," Mia told him. "I wonder if it's something from the old days, a place to hide people and valuables during an attack? From what I understand, Jack Addison, the original owner, was indeed likely to have someone after him or his money."

"That's how I heard it, too," Hank said. "Man was a scoundrel, through and through." He pointed to the flashlight on the table. "That's not Jack's, though, unless he's haunting the place. Someone has been down here recently." He nodded to the old door with new screws. "Kind of a gray area if it's part of the current crime scene or not. I can get a search warrant, but it'd take some time. Got any objections to me opening this?"

"On the contrary, I would have an objection to you not opening that door as soon as possible," Mia told him. "I'm dying to see what's behind it. And perhaps these two gentlemen would like to help? They have experience with this type of work."

Fat chance getting the archaeologists out of there, the sheriff thought, but politely said, "That'll be fine, ma'am." They might as well help.

214

Ed was already prying at the door, trying to open it. "It's locked on the other side, I think."

Sam joined him on the other side, trying to force the door open or part of it apart.

"Why would someone lock it?" Nathan wondered. "No one else knew it was here."

"We don't know that," Hank told him. He shone his flashlight at the rectangular opening in the beamed ceiling. "It looks like a hidden trap door led down here."

Ed commented, "Those stairs were probably fine before the fire." He pointed to a pile of charred lumber on the side of the room.

"Good eyes, Ed." Mia had missed the fragments of crosspieces indicating stairs. "So they could hide down here, and no one would guess they were here."

Hank agreed, "This would be under Misty's stall. She's real gentle, wouldn't hurt a fly." He shook his head. "No wonder Becky had so much trouble keeping the horse thief out. They were inside."

"Misty would have to be incredibly laid back to not care about a stairway opening in her stall," Nathan commented. "I think I would jump a foot, personally, if the floor suddenly opened in the night."

"She was one of the first horses stolen," Sam said. "Poor old Misty."

Ed found a pry bar in the pile of rusted tools. "Okay to use this?" He waved it in the air.

"Go for it," Hank told him.

With a piercing creak followed by a ripping

noise, the doorway opened. Ed shoved what was left of it to the side with his boot.

"A tunnel. Well, what do you know?" Hank said. They all peered down the long tunnel, curious, but a little daunted by the pitch-black nothingness. "Sure is dark down there."

"What do you think, Ed?" Mia asked the excavation expert. "Is it safe to go down? Will the ceiling hold?"

Ed shone his flashlight into the darkness and walked a few steps in. The light crept into the tunnel, never far enough to see much. Roofing timbers and supports made inky shadows, framing the dark. "Seems okay. I mean, I wouldn't get tour groups down here yet, but we should be fine as long as we don't move the supports." He patted one of the side beams.

Sheriff Hank stepped in front of Mia with a polite order of, "Why don't I go first?"

Mia gladly let him, hesitantly stepping into the darkness. She followed the group closely, trying to keep up with the pools of light from those who had flashlights. Sam winked at her and waved a flashlight. "I picked mine up when I got you, Aunt Mia. Want to share?" He thoughtfully placed the puddle of light where she could see where she was stepping.

"Thanks, Sam."

Brightly illuminated spots showed dark, hand-hewn beams holding up the ceiling. Their movement stirred up dust, but not too much, as if this was a well-traveled path, used to plodding feet. The air smelled like rocks and dirt, not musty. Their footsteps echoed oddly in the long tunnel. When she turned back, she couldn't see where they had entered the tunnel. It was an odd feeling to be trapped in the dark inside the feeble light of the flashlight. Mia shivered.

"Well, look at this," Ed's voice called from up ahead. "That hasn't been here long." Lights coalesced next to the tunnel wall.

Mia hurried to see what they were looking at. Aluminum cases reflected the flashlights, dully gleaming against the dirt wall. "I wonder what that could be?" she said aloud. "They couldn't have been here long."

"I think we're about to find out," Sheriff Hank said. He carefully opened the top case, gingerly using his bandanna to preserve fingerprints.

Inside, a red pot covered in beautifully drawn zigzag patterns lay nestled in foam cushions. "I guess we've found the loot." He carefully closed the case and locked it with a sharp click.

"I hope it's all there, especially that lovely flute," Mia said. "Then we can hold the opening next weekend as planned."

"Aunt Mia!" Sam remonstrated.

"Well, we'll see about that when it comes time," Hank broke in. "I think we'll open the rest of these cases when we're back above ground. I'll need my guys to take some photos and dust for fingerprints before we move them." Sheriff Hank pulled out his phone and held it up, then shook his head ruefully. "Not a chance of coverage." He looked ahead into the darkness of the unknown tunnel. "The stolen items should be safe enough here for the time being. Let's see where this leads." He led the way with his measured pace, his light keeping time with his steps.

They followed him, Ed and Nathan quickly, and Sam solicitously guiding his aunt, even though he obviously itched to be exploring in front. The tunnel stretched a long way under the desert floor. It was dry and dusty and completely silent except for their echoing footsteps. Mia wanted to go back down the tunnel and open those cases, find out whether all the stolen antiquities were safely found. She also wanted to know what was at the end of this tunnel. She had a suspicion, but she wouldn't know until she saw it.

They had been walking through the dark for at least ten minutes, doggedly following the puddles of light ahead, when Hank called out, "Another door!"

The passage ended in a trapdoor in the ceiling, reached by stairs bearing marks of recent repairs.

"The end of the tunnel," Ed hurried to examine the trap door, still swinging his pry bar. "Need this?" Hank wordlessly held out his hand, and he handed it to the sheriff.

The door was old wood, like the entrance under the stable. Mia noticed a large rusted iron bar on the platform next to it and heavy brackets to slot the bar into. Anyone on this side could bar the tunnel to someone on the other side. It would take a lot of force to get past that bar, even half rusted through.

Hank placed the tip in the crack of the trap door, then, as an afterthought, looked back at Mia. "Do I have your permission, Miz Mia?"

"Absolutely." She watched curiously as he cracked open the door. They climbed out into what had to be the spirit room at the main hotel.

Hand weavings drooped down the walls, pockmarked from moths and faded with age. A sunken conversation area in the center of the room was piled high with dubious native rugs. A brass incense burner still emitted a distinct patchouli aroma from its prominent dais in the center of the room. Small tables with random spiritual objects cluttered the higher ground. Mia counted at least three corroded metal gongs in different sizes, none of which looked remotely Native American. A Buddha huddled forlornly on the floor at the far end, unpolished and neglected. Shrouded lamps dimly illuminated a few objects in the windowless room; the rest thankfully lay in darkness. A disordered procession of candles, wax gobs dribbling down yellowed wax, ringed the room.

The time capsule of a room was not one Mia thought she'd ever see in a Spinel hotel. A thin layer of dust coated everything. Evidently, the cleaners didn't bother much in here, with good reason. She couldn't imagine why a guest would come in here, and they certainly wouldn't linger. Except for Destiny. She moved a faded tarot card set back next to a crazed crystal ball and sneezed, the sound echoing in the gloomy room.

Sam said in a slightly squeaky voice, "Wow, we're back at the hotel." He coughed and in a deliberately deeper tone, added, "That's a long tunnel."

"Amazing craftsmanship in those days," Ed

commented. "Straight to the hotel. Quicker than we could walk it by the road. Perfect for a rainy day stable entrance." He looked around the room. "It'd be a great idea to add some more tunnels around the hotel, Mia." He grinned, "Just let us know where to dig next."

"We could tunnel under the whole place," Nathan tipped his hat back, looking around the odd room. "You could have tunnels leading all over the property, never have to go outside when it's raining. Nice and cool underground, too."

"I think we're fine with only the one tunnel," Mia told them. "But thank you for the offer."

"Just let us know," Ed said enthusiastically. "Nothing better than building tunnels."

Sheriff Hank said, "This must be the pioneer version of a panic room. Seems pretty well thought out." He fiddled with the cracked trap door frame, trying to see how the hidden door opened from this side. "I wonder if the original house had a hidden entrance to this room from the main hall. Lots of paneling in the building to hide doors in. You'd never know it was here, then. That would be two levels of security."

Peeking behind a large gong, Mia noticed some new, state-of-the-art, modern speaker and mini stereo. "Look at this," she said.

The sheriff came over. "Looks like that's not been here long." He leaned down and pressed play. Immediately, an undulating cry burst their eardrums. He quickly turned it off.

Sam whistled. "I guess maybe Destiny had

other things to do besides yodel when she was in here."

"I guess you're right," the sheriff agreed. "Not enough to arrest her, though."

There was a light knock at the door, and Atsa softly said, "Um, is anyone in there?" She didn't sound like she actually wanted to find anyone.

Sheriff Hank put a finger to his lips, and they all froze, not making a sound.

Atsa tried the doorknob, not very hard. "Is anyone there?" she said in a loud whisper. Then, in a louder tone, obviously retreating, "That room's locked for renovation, Mrs. Tims. I guess something fell and made that noise. Nothing to worry about." Her voice fell away.

"What's next?" Sam whispered.

"We stay very quiet," Mia told him. "We don't want the hospitality team to think there's a ghost in here."

"Everyone already thinks it's pretty weird," Sam commented. "No wonder they call it the spirit room. Perfect fit." He looked around at the random assortment of spiritual objects from the past. "Look at all this junk."

"We still don't want people to know we've found another entrance," Mia told him.

"Or the thief knows we've found their little hidey-hole," the sheriff added.

"I bet it's Destiny," Sam said darkly. "She's always in here."

"She does seem very anxious about this room," Mia agreed. "But we need proof."

"And we'll get it tonight," the sheriff said.

10

To Catch a Thief

When Mia returned to the hotel, she tracked Atsa down at the concierge desk. "Hello, Atsa. Can you please tell me what activities Destiny has planned for today?"

"Hi, Ms. Mia," Atsa replied, an understanding look on her face. "Trying to avoid running into her? I can't blame you." She rapidly tapped at her computer.

"On the contrary, I'm trying to join an activity she's in," Mia told her, watching for Atsa's reaction.

Mia was not disappointed. Atsa looked up in a quick, startled motion of utter disbelief, then her brow smoothed. "Is she your murder suspect?" she asked in a hushed voice. "She is odd," her eyes rolled, illustrating the understatement. "Do you really think she killed Kyle Lee?"

"I just want to find out a little more about her," Mia said evasively.

"Does it have to do with what's going on at the stables?" Atsa asked curiously. "Someone said there were a lot of police cars out there again. I didn't have time to find out on my break." She screwed up her face in disappointment.

Mia answered, "Something along those lines. Are a lot of people asking?"

"Just one or two who'd been on a hike."

"Tell them the fire inspector had a fall while he was investigating the fire. That's the truth and all they need to know right now."

Atsa's dark eyes shone brightly. "But not the whole truth, is it?"

"I'll fill you in on the details later," Mia promised.

Atsa sighed in frustration at being left out. "Is Mr. Graves okay?"

"You do know everyone in town, don't you?" Mia commented with approval. "He's going to be fine, but has a badly broken leg."

"That's too bad," Atsa said. "We always do the county children's cookout on the hotel grounds. Makes it an adventure for the kids." She grinned. "Mr. Graves mans the grills. Wow, that man can cook. He's mastered the grills like Aunt Chooli does her kitchen." She looked with sudden concern at Mia. "Will the hotel do the cookout this year? I mean, I guess because we've always done it, it doesn't mean you have to keep hosting it."

"Plan on it being here," Mia told her. "I think involvement in the local community is part of what makes a great hotel—not a cookie-cutter one. Any ideas you come up with, please tell me." She coughed,

"About those activities."

"Oh, yeah, right," Atsa efficiently scanned the screen. "An advanced climbing lesson is probably not in your plans this trip," she smiled, tucking her glossy black braid behind her shoulder.

"I think not." Mia raised one delicately penciled eyebrow.

"Hot air balloon ride this morning, she's already left for it, back in an hour," Atsa continued. "Cooking class with Chef Chooli, my aunt's going to love that. Destiny drives her nuts. In and out of the kitchen every time she visits. But no one has time for talking during one of my aunt's classes. She keeps them running." She looked up, "Guided Mindful Stress Mastery in the Labyrinth this afternoon. That's perfect. Everyone will be talking about the stuff that's bothering them. You can investigate all you want and blend in."

"Mindful Stress?" Mia said doubtfully.

Atsa shrugged, shifting her feet. "I guess you realize your stressors, so you can control your stress. Not have it get to you so much." She sounded unconvinced as well. "My grandmother always says worry comes from fear. Once you accept the glorious abundance and love around you, there's no reason to be scared anymore of anything. So no stress." She tugged at the end of her braid. "Works for me."

"Your grandmother sounds like a wise woman." Mia could not imagine living life in enough fear to cause constant stress, but she knew people often did. "I'd like to meet her while I'm here. Maybe dinner one night?"

"I know she'd like that. I'll see when she's free," Atsa said with a smile. Her hand hovered over her keyboard. "So Mindful Stress Mastery then?"

"That's all the options?"

Atsa nodded.

"Then stress it is." Mia pinched her arm muscles demonstratively, "I don't think I'm up to climbing today."

Atsa's wide red mouth relaxed in a grin. "Not many people are up to the advanced climbing class. I was sore for a week after the last one I took. Destiny must be in amazing shape, since she's gone twice this week already. Most people need more downtime." She tapped. "Okay, you're signed up. Just show up at the Labyrinth at six o'clock. Prepare to leave all your stress behind," she added, grinning.

"That I can do," Mia said with a laugh. "And here's a step to get rid of some stress." She went past the desk to the manager's door. "Mr. Lagarto? I'd like a word with you."

He looked blearily at her, rubbing his eyes. "What do you want now? You have more ways to ruin my hotel?"

"The hotel is no longer your problem, Mr. Lagarto. You're fired," Mia told him.

That jolted him awake, "You can't fire me," he told her. "You're not the Spinel CEO. You're just some busybody retiree who doesn't know when she's too old to matter."

Mia ignored his personal comment. Firing

people was always unpleasant. "Mr. Lagarto, if you choose to confirm your dismissal with Mr. Mark Spinel, you'll hear exactly the same as I just told you, but I doubt he'll be so polite. You are fired."

He heaved himself out of the chair with a harsh creak. "I guess I'll have to take your word for it." He opened his desk drawer, looking in, then said, "It's too much trouble to sort through this stuff. Just have the staff pack it up and drop it off."

"Mr. Spinel will mail you your severance check and other information. You should receive them within two days," Mia told him.

He nodded ponderously, oily skin glistening in the dim light. "I'll have to get my brother-in-law to give me my old job at his car lot again. Hated working there, but better than a place with a murderer running loose."

"I'm glad you feel that way," Mia said sincerely.

She followed him out of the room, closing the door behind her.

He didn't bother to say goodbye to Atsa or anyone else on his way out, just trudged across the lobby and out the door, not even glancing behind him.

Mia looked at Atsa. "Mr. Lagarto is no longer employed by this hotel."

"It's about time," Atsa said, relieved. "Who's the new manager?"

"Mark has it down to several excellent candidates. I'll fill in for a few weeks until they can transfer here." Mia shook her head. "It just wasn't worth putting up with him anymore."

"There aren't any assistant managers," Atsa told her. "They left before the renovations, and Mr. Lagarto never hired replacements. Said it was a waste of money."

"I know," Mia told her. "Are you interested in being an assistant manager?"

Atsa looked eager for a minute, then frowned. "I wish I could, but school." She sighed and tugged hard on her braid. "I just can't."

"Try it," Mia urged. "At the very least, help me manage for a few weeks and get the raise that goes with the extra work. We can work with your schedule so you're not overwhelmed. School always comes first, but we can arrange your hours around classes."

"I don't know," Atsa said hesitantly.

"Try it. Then, when the new manager arrives, you can decide what you want to do." Mia smiled at her, "I think we can make it work, but there's no harm in trying it. Besides, we're going to need someone who knows astronomy to oversee the observatory construction and programs. And we have several scholarship programs you might be interested in," Mia added, with a distinct attempt at bribery.

"Okay," Atsa said slowly. "Okay, I think I will."

"Good. Then your first job is to find another concierge. This desk is woefully understaffed," Mia ordered. "Do you know anyone who would do a good job?"

"Yeah, one of the trail guides is fantastic. Really gets people enthusiastic about activities."

"Sounds perfect," Mia said crisply. "Set up an

interview for me. And, Atsa," she paused, "I want to officially put the people in charge who have actually been running the hotel—and running it very well, I must say. I think you can guide me on that."

Atsa blushed beet red.

"Next, ship Mr. Lagarto's things to him and get that dreadful room cleaned." She shuddered, reflexively wiping her hands on her pants. "I think things are living in that desk. I need a working office."

"Yes, ma'am," Atsa gave her a mock salute. "And after that?"

"Work out a reasonable schedule for yourself. I expect the evening shift will coordinate the best with school."

"I think I can do that," Atsa said. "Thanks, Ms. Mia."

"Thank you, Atsa."

The Labyrinth nestled in a beautiful setting— not too far from the main hotel, yet surrounded by mountains and orange groves. Blood red stones guided the classic path, weaving around a central circle, where a tall fire blazed in a bronze vessel. Flames leaped, casting dancing light on the class members. Small, thoughtfully placed rocks served as seating around the large circle. The air smelled hot and primitive, mingled dust and fire.

Mixed expressions surrounded her, some wary,

some heartbreakingly hopeful, and some simply, as Atsa had said, scared. It was difficult to go through life without any fear at all, but almost impossible to live always crippled by fear, Mia thought. Tension twanged like a bowstring in the little group. The anxiety and worry in these people, how could the instructor possibly lift any of that burden?

The teacher's face remained serenely peaceful. Gray yoga clothes fitted like they were part of her. Her long, silvery braid reached halfway down her back and shone like a golden aureole in the setting sun. Smiling in greeting to the participants, she told them, "Welcome," her voice sonorous like a ringing bell.

A little uncertain shuffling, no one knowing quite how to respond to the single word. Mia took advantage of the movement to place herself squarely next to Destiny. Destiny had closed her eyes and swayed meditatively side to side, her long frizzy hair moving to an inner beat. Mia hadn't seen the instructor tell her to do that, but perhaps Destiny had taken the class before, and swaying was the first step.

A late participant, Emily, came running into the group, quickly quieting her jarring arrival and whispering in a penetrating tone, "Sorry, sorry, everyone." She wiped her forehead with her sleeve.

Destiny opened her eyes and glared at Emily, her body suddenly still and tense.

Mia gave Emily an encouraging smile, which she returned with a token movement of her lips. Emily had been under a great deal of stress, between the documentary and her ex-boyfriend's death. Maybe this class would help her.

The teacher continued, each word carefully enunciated in resonant tones, firelight gleaming in her silver hair, "Life holds many reasons to stress and worry, some common to all of us and some unique to each individual here." A wide smile of radiant joy spread across her face. "In this class, you will accept each reason you have to stress, accept the burden that stress has caused you, then learn to toss that burden away, like a shoe that no longer fits, so it is no longer needed."

"Living with complete mastery of stress is possible, but it is a lifelong skill, which with discipline becomes easier to do with time and practice. We will take the first steps on your journey tonight."

The teacher's bright gray eyes searched the individuals in her class. "Anyone who feels comfortable, now speak briefly of what is causing your worry and why you want to leave that worry behind." She nodded to Destiny. "What is your stress?"

Destiny smoothed her long necklace of beads and tossed her cloud of hair back over her shoulders. "My stress is my business," she answered contemptuously. She glared at the teacher, daring her to pry further.

"Of course." The teacher smoothly moved on to a small, elderly woman. "What burden do you want to lift today?"

The diminutive woman smiled, a little ruefully. "I take care of my grandchildren quite often. It's wonderful to have them, but I need to have a bit more patience to deal with them."

The class laughed in shared understanding, and the teacher added, "So would we all. Patience is a hard thing to come by with active children." She continued going around the group, kindly asking each person what burden they hoped to ease.

When the teacher came to Mia, she realized she had been so interested in everyone else's replies that she had forgotten to think up a potential stress to explain her presence in the class. Quickly realizing the last thing she wanted to do in front of guests was mention the theft and murder, she said, "I have missed my husband since his death." The teacher nodded in sympathy and moved on.

Mia, with slight surprise at the words that had come out of her mouth, realized it was the truth. She missed her husband, Leo, very much right now. They had always solved problems, like hotel thefts, but never murders, together, both contributing knowledge and complementary viewpoints. While she valued the help of Sam and Atsa, she very much missed the deep wisdom her husband always showed when a problem came up. She felt a tear welling up and tamped it firmly down. This was no moment for weakness. She was going to clear up this dreadful crime and prevent it from happening again. Leo would never have tolerated a murder at his hotel without finding the murderer and seeing that they were punished for their crime. Well, Leo wasn't here. It was up to her to clean up this mess. She coughed once, clearing herself of any possible tears.

Leaning over, Destiny told her, in a softer tone than Mia had heard her use, "I'm sorry about your husband."

"Thank you."

"I recently lost someone I cared about, too," she continued quietly, stroking her long strand of turquoise beads.

"I am so sorry," Mia said, commiserating.

"It's harder than you'd think, looking from the outside, to lose someone you love." Destiny's eyes welled up with tears.

"It is," Mia agreed. "I never thought I'd lose him so suddenly," she choked a little, remembering that terrible day her husband died and her life changed forever.

"One minute you're laughing and making plans together. The next, you know you'll never see them again." Destiny withdrew a little, tugging on her necklace and tucking her hair back.

"It is very hard," Mia gave her the space she clearly needed. She watched the teacher slowly make her way around the small group, listening to each concern with equal care. Mia approved of that. After all, someone's job decision may not seem as meaningful as the death of a loved one, but to the person experiencing the worry over an important choice, it was the center of their current life.

She watched curiously as the teacher circled around to Emily. Would Emily mention Kyle's death? Or was her job stress topmost in her mind?

Emily shuffled her feet a little, then looked up. "I recently lost someone I cared about," she said quietly. She shoved her brown hair out of her eyes, then hung her head a little, looking into the dancing flames in the center of the labyrinth.

The teacher stood in front of the fire, her silver hair golden in the firelight and setting sun. "We've all accepted our greatest stress. Now, it's time to master it so you can enjoy the full abundance of life." She held out her hands in supplication. "Stress does not disappear in the blink of an eye. Some concerns are constant, part of life. Some will recede in time or in proportion, but there will always be another to take their place."

"Then what's the point of this?" Destiny muttered.

The teacher's melodious voice cut in like a flute solo, "The point is your stress does not have to overwhelm you. You can learn to live without the constant anxiety and fear from that stress. You can master it, in time."

She looked around the class. "So you've identified your greatest stressor. You've acknowledged the power it has over you. Now, as you walk the labyrinth, put it away. Take that power back. Accept it without fear and worry. If you do think about your stress from a place of fear, continue your walk. When you feel ready, join me at the heart of the maze, next to the fire."

She motioned people to several different entrances around the large labyrinth. "Take each step slowly. Listen to the sound of your footfall, enjoy the movement, take joy in the world around you. Experience the moment you're in." She paused a minute, noticing several students who seemed lost. "Don't worry if you think of your stress. Worrying about stress just adds to the burden!" She grimaced. "Not what we're going for. Just keep moving through the circle until you feel ready to step into the center. You can always come back tomorrow and practice more. When you feel ready, you're ready."

Mia started walking, the sun glowing red on the stones guiding her. She didn't need to think about Leo as a stress. Thoughts of him were always calming.

She heard the gravel rolling with tiny clattering noises beneath her feet. She tried to walk more quietly, and her foot made a silky gliding sound, moving through the desert sand. This was very unlike walking in the tunnel. The tunnel floor had been dug deeper, much deeper, down to hard sandstone and red iron-rich dust. The first thing she had done after walking under the ground had been to take a long shower. The red mud streaming down the drain had looked like blood so much that she had searched for an open wound. But it was all just mud, going down the drain.

Mia took another careful step, feeling the sandy gravel shifting under her feet. Why had Kyle had to die? Soft whispers of the sand sinking beneath her feet were her only answer. She knew who had killed Kyle, but not why. Nothing seemed like an adequate motive to take a life.

Mia moved slowly toward the center of the Labyrinth, hearing the other footsteps converging together. To her surprise, the sun had set during her long journey through the maze. The only light now was the flickering firelight.

The teacher greeted all who arrived with a brief bow of her head at a task well done. With solemn faces, they huddled close around the fire, hot on their faces after the cold desert night winding through the maze. When all had assembled around the primitive bronze bowl holding the flames, the teacher smiled. "And now, it's time for the final step."

Mia wondered if she'd throw some herb bundle into the flames, symbolically ridding them of their stress and creating fragrant, or not so sweet, smoke. Or maybe circle the fire and chant. She started to yawn, changing into a chuckle at the teacher's finale.

"I brought marshmallows!" the teacher said with a joyful laugh. She held up a bowl and some long toasting forks. "Anyone who wants s'mores, the chocolates and graham crackers are over there."

The class laughed with her, all taking their marshmallows and toasting them over the open flames. Stress forgotten, the firelight danced on delighted smiles, sticky fingers, and pure joy.

Mia walked slowly back to her cottage, breathing in the glorious fragrance of the orange trees. She was only slightly startled when she saw Neal Mjesec, where they'd met before. He stood stock still, gazing wistfully up at the sky where he'd seen Sam's 'UFO.'

As she came up, he turned to her with an eager smile. "Have you seen our friends again?"

She shook her head. "I'm afraid not, Neal."

"That's too bad." His long face drooped. "I hoped they would land soon and everyone could see the truth for themselves." He twisted his fingers together and visibly sagged, like a marionette collapsing.

"If they're scouting, it's possible they picked another location," Mia suggested, trying to cheer him up. "Or perhaps they'll be back," she added with reluctance.

Neal's face brightened. "After all, we don't know what time scale they're working with. It might be a thousand years." He slipped on the hill slightly, stretching out one gangly leg for balance.

"Aliens would come from very far away," Mia told him. "It could be decades before they return, if then. They might choose another location or even another planet."

"I know," Neal agreed disconsolately. "I just wish I could see them one more time. Just to see they're out there. I've spent so much time chasing down rumors that it would mean a lot to me to see them clearly. Sometimes, simply knowing they're out there isn't enough." His yearning eyes searched the dark blue bowl of the sky. Tiny stars glittered in the endless night, bright pinpoints like glittering diamonds. "There are so many solar systems out there for them. Why should they pick ours?" His mouth turned down, like a disappointed child's, and his shoulders crumpled inward.

"I hope you do see them," Mia told him sincerely. "But there are too many charlatans in this world, so I hope you also investigate each incident thoroughly. Many are probably fake."

"I know, I got very excited two nights ago," Neal told her, "But it turned out to be just a person in the desert."

The night of the theft and murder, Mia thought with sudden interest, but merely said, "What were they doing?"

"Just running through the desert," Neal told her. "They were holding a red flashlight, so it looked like it could be aliens, you know?" He coughed with embarrassment. "I was only fooled for a minute." He sighed. "Red lights help prevent night blindness."

"An unexpected red light in the desert at night is unusual," Mia said with understanding. "It would have tricked me, too."

"It was that tall woman with the beads," Neal told her. "Destiny." He pinched his long, narrow nose and compressed his lips. "I see her in the desert a lot at night. Always looks like she's in a hurry to go somewhere, even in the middle of nowhere." He compressed his neck a little, like a long-necked turtle withdrawing into its shell, then warily stretched out a little. "I've wondered what she was up to here because I know something about her." He looked hesitant, clearly wondering whether to say anything.

"You do? I've been curious," Mia gently encouraged.

"Well, it was back a few years, but she used to

have a spiritual shop in Los Angeles. Still has it, I guess."

"A spiritual shop?" Mia asked curiously.

"A hodgepodge with a bit of everything that could be metaphysical. Indian artifacts, Tibetan Buddhas, peace pipes, fake Egyptian scarabs, crystals, lots of candles, and incense." Neal screwed up his nose. "The whole place reeked with the smell." He shifted his weight on his long legs, "The more expensive items were seen by invitation only in the back room. Authentic Anasazi pottery, nothing like the front area's made last Tuesday, factory stuff. Some really beautiful Japanese porcelain and a lovely little Egyptian scarab," he sighed wistfully. "Most of that room was too expensive for my wallet back then. There were a few pieces I wish I could buy now, even knowing better."

"What do you mean, knowing better?"

"I got involved because a friend was buying some alien artifacts for a pretty hefty price. Worth it to him if they're real, but he wanted to check. So I did some radiation and cosmogenic nuclide tests and found there is no way those artifacts were ever in outer space. Saved my friend a lot of money. Destiny apologized a ton, and I assumed she'd been conned into buying fakes." He shrugged. "Once I knew the alien artifacts were fakes, the next time I went in that back room, I examined the lot. I found out Destiny had several stolen objects in there, not just fakes. I told her, thinking I was helping an honest shop owner who'd been tricked." He grimaced and stretched one leg behind the other in an awkward crane pose. "I couldn't have been more wrong."

"What did she say?"

"She said if I went to the authorities or mentioned it to anyone, she'd sue me for slander. My friend had bought a few pieces, and he'd go to jail for buying stolen goods. She even said she'd accuse me of selling her some of the stolen pieces." His voice rose to a high squeak. "Me!"

"My goodness," Mia exclaimed. "That's terrible."

His voice returned to normal. "Of course, I know now that I should have gone straight to the police, and the rest of it was just empty threats." He shook his head at his naivety. "But back then, I was terrified. I was in my first real job, you know, and frightened she'd call my boss and have me fired, like she threatened."

"I can see why."

"So I kept my mouth shut and didn't go within a block of her store again," Neal concluded. "I doubt she even remembers me. It's been a long time, and I was just a kid." He shook his head. "A really naive kid."

Mia said thoughtfully, "With all that's happened here, Destiny having some doubtful antiquity dealings in her past might be significant."

"Yeah, I thought it might be pretty relevant," Neal said with a wry smile. "I didn't want to tell the police or anyone official, you know? It was so long ago, and I don't have any proof at all. It's all just hearsay at this point. My friend died last year, so I don't have anyone to back up my story."

"I understand," Mia said. "Well, I can mention it as a rumor to the sheriff, if you'd like? I'll have to say you told me if I have to testify about it, but if it's just a nudge in the right direction for him, I don't suppose it would ever come up."

Neal said with relief, "That sounds best. Thanks, Mia." He looked like a heavy weight had gone off his shoulders as he slowly straightened up. "I've been worried about it since the murder."

"You're very welcome, Neal." She frowned a little. "There is still one big question, though."

"What's that?" he asked.

"What is Destiny doing running around the desert at night?"

He switched his crane stance to the other leg. "Maybe looking for antiquities?"

"If we found the flute, there might be something else? That's possible, I suppose," Mia said doubtfully. "Did you ever come to this resort in the old days, back when Destiny knew the owners?"

"No," Neal said curiously. "Do you think she knows something about the hotel from them?"

"I'm not sure," Mia said. "She seems to turn up in a lot of unexpected places."

"I'll tell you if I see her again on the grounds at night," Neal promised.

"Thank you," Mia told him. "Good night."

"Good night."

Sneaking into the Spirit Guide room that night sounded much easier than it actually was. They had a cunningly simple plan. One of the police officers would ask James to meet him for a moment outside while their little group snuck into the room.

It wasn't that simple.

As Mia slipped out of her hiding place, James was called back inside by another phone call. And there was Mia, standing in the middle of the lobby.

Mia, unable to think of a reason for wandering around the hotel at night, simply didn't give one. Understandably curious, James chatted, hoping to discover why Mia had appeared in the lobby at this late hour. Since James didn't show up outside, the police officer came to find him. James was reluctant to leave his desk unattended while the hotel owner was overseeing him. After much urging by Mia, James went to see the excuse the police officer had concocted.

Sheriff Hank whispered, "Okay, move it," and practically shoved the rest of the group out of the little alcove they'd crowded into. They quickly escaped into the Spirit Guide room with heartfelt relief.

It had been tricky for Mia and Sam to get a front row seat tonight, but Sheriff Hank had relented on the grounds that, "It would be a heck of a lot more trouble to get a warrant than to just let you sit in a corner."

Partially hidden behind a massive bronze gong, Mia and Sam waited quietly. At least, Mia sat still. Sam constantly shifted, scraping the floor with his shoe and creaking the chair, but none of his noises were loud enough to be heard outside the room. She hoped.

The sheriff had fixed the hidden trap door panel so that the damage was unnoticeable. Looking prepared for a long, dull night, he crouched against the far wall with his deputy, waiting to see who entered and if they knew about the secret tunnel. If so, Hank had his thief—and his murderer. They had made entry easy for the murderer, with James regularly called away from the front desk—and a hidden officer watching for his safety. The two men were absolutely still, hunters waiting for their prey.

The overwhelming silence of the room felt isolated and airless, every breath stirring floating dust motes. Sam's shoe shuffling on the floor hollowly echoed against the bedraggled tapestries. As her eyes adjusted to the dark, the room's idols became monstrous, stuff out of nightmares instead of tacky spiritualist paraphernalia. Dragons on one wall twisted and turned just at the corner of her eye. The big bronze Buddha's serene smile morphed into a malevolent grin. A crystal skull, shrouded by dust, winked at her, refracted light flickering deep inside. A massive granite altar against one wall, benignly tawdry by light, seemed to ooze viscous dark liquid from its pores.

During the long hours, Mia wondered who would enter the Spirit Guide Room. The others were sure Destiny was the culprit, especially after Mia repeated Neal's story, which definitely implicated her in antiquity thefts.

Mia wasn't so sure. Destiny, with her knowledge of the ranch and selling stolen goods, must be involved in the thefts, but she didn't think Destiny was the murderer. Her shock and grief at the Labyrinth had seemed genuine, unlike her usual facade. In the dusky gloom, Mia turned over each of the suspects in her head.

She liked Neal, but he admitted knowledge of museum thefts, which, at the least, he hadn't reported. Alien hunting would make a very believable cover story for him to be around at unusual places and times. The archaeologists certainly hadn't been digging legally when she found them. Who knew what illegal activities they were party to? From their little dinner party, the Wallaces knew Destiny a lot better than initial appearances suggested. Mia didn't know why they would lie about knowing someone, even a dealer in dubious antiquities, unless they were buying stolen objects under the table. That skull Kyle had supposedly stolen had actually been found in Pete's camera bag. And Emily had packed all of the bags.

As the door creaked open, emitting a bright shaft of light, Mia placed her hand on Sam's shoulder, stilling him. Two shadowy figures entered the room and quickly closed the door behind them, leaving the room in darkness again. A tiny penlight flickered, pointing down at the floor and briefly spotlighting the room. Thankfully, none of the watchers were seen in the brief reconnaissance, and the light moved back to the floor.

"Keep moving," the figure in back ordered the taller shape in a harsh whisper.

"I'm moving, I'm moving," said Destiny, in a squeak of her normal voice. "I just don't want to trip on the stairs." Her tall figure stumbled a little, jerking to one side and righting herself.

"You have enough light to see by, even with all this junk in the way. Keep moving, or I will shoot you," the figure hissed. "Get that tunnel open."

Obviously terrified, Destiny scuttled across the room, making a beeline for the secret tunnel entrance. Tripping over a rug fringe, she went down with a loud crash, falling flat on her face. A brass candlestick clanged, slowly rattling to a stop.

"That's it," the other figure said, in a furious whisper. Light reflected on her face, revealing Emily, transformed from an inefficient assistant to a very efficient predator. "I've had enough of you and your incompetence." She kicked at Destiny's face, preventing her from rising. "I have a much better plan." Emily's lips moved into a wide, cruel smile. It didn't reach her eyes.

"Please." Destiny tried to rise again. Emily pushed her down with her foot, still smiling.

"You're going to take the blame for Kyle's death. Tragically, you commit suicide because you killed your lover." She looked around at the dated spiritual remnants. "Everyone knows how much you love this rubbish heap of a room. What a perfect place for you to end it all." She laughed, very softly.

"You killed him!" Destiny was shocked. "You killed him because he wanted to be with me, not you. I could never kill anyone," she added virtuously. She struggled to rise, and Emily kicked her down.

"Yeah, right, you're completely innocent.

Remember, I know all about your business," Emily scoffed. "And you're digging in the caves here illegally. You really thought you could find buried treasure from those old maps?"

"I did find it!" Destiny protested. "I just haven't found much this trip."

"And all the other Anasazi pottery is long gone to the highest bidder, huh?" Emily laughed bitterly. "Too bad you didn't find that flute instead of some construction worker."

"I've found a lot of things," Destiny shot back, stung. "They're just guarding the horses more. I can't exactly dig when people are watching."

"Because it's theft," Emily chortled. She waved the gun like a parade flag. "You're a thief, like me. You're just not as good at it."

"At least I'm not a murderer!" Destiny accused, then, realizing what she'd said, riveted her eyes on the gun. Her eyes followed the barrel as Emily slowly moved it back and forth, shaking her head.

"Anyway, I didn't kill Kyle because he was with you," Emily informed her. "I killed him because I was sick and tired of him taking most of the money from our projects while I did most of the work." She looked around the room, clearly planning Destiny's death. "Isn't there a ritual knife around here somewhere?" She backed away a little, shining her penlight on the nearest tables with a quick darting motion.

"Kyle planned the thefts, not you!" Destiny started to get off the floor, gathering herself to attack Emily.

Emily moved quickly, shoving her down while holding the gun on her the entire time. "Is that what he told you?" she sneered. "Sounds like you would believe just about anything, like your credulous customers." She waved the gun, an annoying finger in Destiny's face. Destiny crouched lower on the floor in submission. "I," she emphasized, "planned the thefts. It was all me." Her smile grew wide as her cold eyes searched the room for the knife. "I caught Kyle on his very first attempt at theft at the museum I worked at." She giggled, a harsh burble in the echoing room. "He'd actually tried to use me to get access to the vaults. I told him there were much better ways than that." She shook her head in disgust. "I didn't even have access to the important vaults. Why did he think I was working at a dump like that in the first place?"

"But he told me," Destiny began.

"Shut up!" Emily ordered, waggling the gun in Destiny's face. "It was all me. My plan from the start. I told him to get me the assistant job with Hal. It was a dream. Open access to absolutely anything I wanted. No one wanted to accuse a film crew of theft without a lot of proof because of bad publicity. All I had to do was get Kyle to film somewhere, and I could steal anything I wanted. All Kyle did was put on his little documentary show—with my research, I might add, find out any security codes I needed and help me carry out the stuff." Emily emphasized her point with a flick of her gun. "Oh, and sell it to you." She grimaced. "You paid lousy prices, considering their worth. Now I'll have to find a new dealer. You're the only one who knows about any of it." She shook her head, "Finding a new dealer will be a real pain, but worth it to get rid of Kyle. He kept screwing up, even with the minimal amount he was supposed to do."

"You killed him for that?" Destiny had forgotten to stay down or be quiet. She was crouching, readying herself to spring, despite the gun.

"He was a leech," Emily coldly stated. "And completely incompetent."

"Why you—" Destiny lunged at Emily, and the gun went off, the noise shattering the silence.

There was scuffling confusion for a brief minute, then Hank's voice rang out, "Sam, flip that confounded light on, will you?"

Sam, grateful for action of any kind, slipped out of his chair, and light shone on a very odd scene.

Destiny held her arm and howled like a banshee. Emily stared around the room, coldly assessing her situation. Her eyes fell on Mia with a venomous fury that made Mia very glad the sheriff was holding on to her.

But not holding hard enough. With a sudden twist and roll to the ground, Emily slipped out of the sheriff's hands and across the room. It only took a moment for her to make it through the trap door. Her scream of impotent rage rattled the room when she couldn't bar the door behind her, then they heard quick running footsteps going down the tunnel. A quick startled scream, and the sheriff called, "Got her?"

"Yeah, but she's a biter." A quick scuffle. "Oh no, you don't." The officer called back, "Got the cuffs on her. She's not getting out of that. I'll take her down to the jail."

"Watch her like a hawk," the sheriff looked at Mia. "Good here?"

Mia already had her phone out, calling an ambulance for Destiny. "Good here."

"I can't believe she killed a man over an old flute," the sheriff said.

Mia didn't reply. There was nothing to say.

A hesitant knock on the door broke the silence. James squeaked uncertainly, "Um, is anybody in there?"

They all laughed.

11

A Grand Opening

Mia swirled her rust-colored silk scarf around her neck, letting it settle into flattering folds. She linked her arm in Sam's, "Off we go," she said gaily.

He gave a little skip and jump that was probably supposed to be a dance move. "Time to celebrate, Aunt Mia," he grinned. Mia had dragged him to be fitted for a tuxedo—which he looked quite dashing in—and from his expression, he knew it.

Controlled chaos enveloped them as soon as they entered the exhibit room. The crowd moved around the room, pinballing from the exhibits to the auction items with cries of "Ooh, beautiful!" and "I'm bidding on that." Satin silks swished past rich velvets and elegant tuxedos. Hands clasped champagne flutes and the reflective prisms of cut crystal whiskey tumblers. Waiters in crisp uniforms swam through the crowd, handing out drinks and delicious appetizer nibbles.

Round dining tables were scattered throughout the room, covered by deep red tablecloths and topped with loose wildflower arrangements in woven baskets Mia had found at a local artisans' collective. Candles burned low, flickering warm yellow in their ironwork holders. Musicians played from one of the balconies, soft flutes harmonizing with tapping drums, suiting the mood of the displayed antiquities.

Tahoma brought her a glass of chilled champagne, discreetly informing her, "The affair seems like a great success, Ms. Mia."

"It was certainly worth all the trouble." Mia and her team had worked until just before the party, restoring the ballroom to its original splendor and the displays to their places.

"It was, indeed. A perfect event to launch our new hotel." Tahoma slipped back into the crowd, smoothing rough edges with his silver platter of drinks.

"It is perfect, isn't it, Sam?" Sam was too busy eyeing a girl in a wisp of a sparkly dress with a bright smile on her face to reply. "Isn't that the girl you were talking to at the pool, Sam?" she asked. "You should go say hello."

He grinned down at her, then was across the room at the girl's side in what Mia considered a respectable race speed.

She noticed Susan Johnson hovered at the edge of the room, clipboard still in hand. Susan wore a simple black dress and the gorgeous blue silk scarf Mia had presented her. She looked around the beautiful room, with a proud smile on her face at the successful event. With a bit of Mia's and the new manager's training, Susan would plan events to remember.

Mia looked around her for someone interesting to talk with and spotted Pete at the edge of the room, looking a little lost at an event without his cameras.

"How are you?" Mia asked.

He looked at her. "It's weird, you know?"

"I would think so." Mia couldn't imagine the shock of having one coworker murdered by another.

"I knew both Kyle and Emily for so long, you know?" Pete shook his head, shaking off illusions. "I thought Kyle was the thief, even talked about how to keep him away from the artifacts with Hal and Emily. Then to find out Emily, sweet little Emily, was the mastermind behind all the thefts." He took a quick gulp of Scotch. "Emily, a murderer and a thief. I liked her, you know. Thought she was a good kid." He shook his head again. "I never would have guessed it."

"She hid her true nature well," Mia told him. Emily's scream of fury from the tunnel still echoed in her head sometimes, in the middle of the night. Emily had been a very different person than she appeared.

"I never did understand why they dated," Pete mused. "Kyle usually went for flashier types, or at least a lot richer." He slowly turned his Scotch glass, looking at the crystal lights flashing through the amber fluid. "I never did understand it."

"I think it turned into a business partnership fairly early in their relationship," Mia said. "Emily was running the entire show, both the production and thefts."

"Did you know it was her?" Pete asked.

"I had an idea she had more to do with the thefts than it seemed," Mia thought back. "She appeared incompetent, but was actually very good at her job, except when little mishaps might smooth the thief's way." She continued, "Emily was the one who packed and unpacked equipment bags, where loot was most likely to be transported. If any artifacts, like the skull, were found, they were in company property where many people had access. But actually, she was usually the only person who handled the equipment."

"She always insisted on lugging those heavy bags," Pete added. "Wouldn't let anyone else do it. We quit offering."

"Carrying lots of bags also gave her multiple trips in and out of buildings. Plenty of opportunities to circumvent door locks or security systems." Mia laughed, "I would guess she could easily remember security codes she saw entered again and again. Or snag a key card from a guard. She added putty to the latch on the fire escape door here, so it wouldn't lock."

"I can't believe she fooled me for that long." Pete downed his Scotch. "Looks like a good party for the museum, at least. The documentary helped pull a lot of potential donors in. That's good."

"I see Richard gloating over the auction numbers so far," Mia agreed. "I expect he will get his exhibit wing out of it."

"That's good," Pete repeated vaguely.

Sheriff Hank entered the room, dressed up in a dark suit with an intricate bolo tie. At his side was

Becky, in much better health than Mia had expected, and dressed in an elegant navy blue sheath. The only outward sign of her recent injury was a thin line of stitches on her forehead. Heading straight for Mia, she said. "Hi, Ms. Mia. Thanks for inviting me."

"It's good to see you, Becky."

"I can't tell you how good it feels to be out of the house," Becky told her. "Hank's been telling me about your adventures." She smiled up at him, her eyes crinkling at the edges.

"Hank was quite the hero," Mia told her.

"He always is," Becky patted his arm. A little shyly, she held out her hand with an exquisite diamond ring adorning it. "We're getting married this summer."

"Congratulations!" Mia couldn't think of a more suited couple.

"Finally getting hitched after all this time," Hank said proudly, encircling her shoulders with his big arm.

"Just took you two years to work up to asking me," Becky laughed up at him, tanned face glowing with happiness.

"You must have the wedding here," Mia told her.

"I thought," Becky started hesitantly. "I thought, maybe at the stables?" She looked hopefully at Mia.

"The new stables?" Mia asked. "Perfect." Her eyes grew dreamy. "Oh, I can just imagine party lights strung all over the stable and along the fence. Big wooden tables piled with a feast and lovely wildflower garlands hanging in the air." She sketched out plans in the air.

Becky smiled, a little uncertainly, at Mia's passionate decorating schemes for her wedding.

Mia continued, "And you need to get Hank to consult on the new stable manager's cottage. If you still want to live there, of course."

"Becky needs to be near her horses," Hank put in, smiling at his future wife. "I don't want her pining away."

Mia smiled benevolently at the two lovebirds and discreetly moved off, so they could discuss their bright future.

She almost didn't recognize Ed and Nathan in their tailored tuxedos, but their enthusiasm for the flute carried across the room. Nathan exclaimed when he saw her, "We've had the perfect idea for the flute."

She delicately lifted her eyebrow, wondering what they'd come up with this time.

"We can get it scanned, inside and out, and make a recreation of the flute. We could hear what it sounds like, without damaging the original."

"What a wonderful idea!" Mia waved Richard over from his observation post, overseeing the silent auction. "Nathan and Ed have had the most lovely idea, Richard."

Humoring her, Richard politely gave the two archaeologists his attention.

"Three-dimensionally scan the flute, then print out replicas," Nathan said enthusiastically. "You could have several different musicians play music on the replicas, so we could hear their concepts of what it would have sounded like."

"I like it. You could even sell models in the gift shop," Richard added, museum funding brightening his eyes. "Kids would love playing what they just saw."

"I'd buy one too," John Wallace said, joining the conversation. "Since it sure doesn't look like I'm getting my hands on the real thing." He laughed.

"I think we've already raised enough to cover the new wing construction," Richard said, his eyes drifting to the bidding table.

"That is wonderful news," Estela enthused. Her deep red gown and ruby and diamond tiara made her look like a queen. "Everything has turned out so well."

"It has, indeed," John agreed. "And I was happy to help Hank catch that Destiny woman peddling her stolen museum pieces. What a piece of work."

"She was the one riding horses at night," Mia added. "Emily was holding back some of her stolen treasures, hoping for better prices and looking for another dealer. Destiny was trying to make up the difference by going through the old ranch maps she'd gotten from her friends, who'd been the hotel owners."

"Surely they couldn't have been buried treasure maps," Ed chuckled. "We've tried a few of those, and they never pan out."

"She thought they were, anyway," Mia said. "We found them hidden away behind a panel in the Spirit Guide Room. Original maps of the ranch, showing where gold mines had been and where they'd found evidence of ancient American habitation. She was searching every location she could get to."

"Those poor horses," Estela murmured.

Richard told her, "As the museum director, I can't thank you enough for all you've done."

"I was glad to help," Mia said, sipping her sparkling champagne with pleasure.

After the party was over, Sam politely accompanied Mia back to her cottage. It was very dark, indeed, and Mia wasn't surprised to run into Neal Mjesec at his usual haunt.

"Hello, Neal," she greeted him. "Have you seen anything?"

"Not since we did, Mia." He looked at her, face drooping in disappointment. "I'm leaving tomorrow, so tonight is my last chance."

From the twist of his mouth, Sam was trying very hard not to laugh. She pinched him hard on the arm, and his face straightened quickly.

"I'm sorry about that, Neal."

"Like you said, we don't have proof of what we saw, but I know it." He put his hand over his heart. "Here, I know that we saw something not of this world. I just wish I could see it one more time." He sighed, collapsing the tripod he had at the ready and packing his camera away, gangly arms making short work of it. Straightening up, he smiled at Mia. "At least you saw it too. That's something."

Sam made a muffled cry. "What's that?"

They all turned and gaped.

A green glow lit up a distant mountain. The glow flickered, then shot a tremendous light column into the air, lingering for just a few seconds before collapsing in on itself. The night was still and dark again. The only lights showing were those of the hotel and stars in the sky.

"What was that?" Sam's mouth hung open, staring at the sky.

"That was a UFO!" Neal said, holding his hand to his chest again. "We saw a UFO!"

"A UFO?" Sam asked. "Really?" His voice was full of wonder. "We saw a UFO?"

"Really," Neal told him with a beaming smile, which quickly faded. "And I forgot to film it again."

"Never mind about that," Mia said. "You saw it. You might not have proof, but you did see it one more time."

"You're right," Neal said enthusiastically. "Two sightings. This has been the best vacation ever!"

"I'm so glad," Mia told him. She looked at Sam's awed face and smiled.

She'd have to thank Nathan and Ed for the special effects tomorrow.

Ms. Mia Murder Mysteries
Lighthearted and Fun Mysteries
with Satisfying Conclusions.

A luxurious private island paradise, with palm trees and white sand beaches, sets the stage for this classic cozy mystery.

A Gilded Age mansion on a secluded Maine island, perched on rocky cliffs overlooking the ocean, sets the scene for a classic murder mystery.

In a sun-drenched tropical paradise, Ms. Mia chases a vanishing corpse and a cunning killer in this delightful cozy murder mystery.

An Italian villa vacation turns deadly—Ms. Mia unmasks a cunning poisoner in this lighthearted cozy murder mystery.

Amid sultry jazz, glittering facades, and long-buried secrets, Ms. Mia untangles a dangerous web of money, loyalty, and betrayal. With wit, charm and a glass of champagne, can Ms. Mia catch the villain before they strike again?

Coming in Summer 2026: Ms. Mia uncovers a deadly plot in Kentucky horse country.

Jennifer Branch writes classic mysteries set in glamorous destinations.

Her Ms. Mia Murder Mysteries follow an elegant amateur sleuth as she uncovers secrets and solves murders at luxurious resorts around the world—from Georgia's Sea Islands and remote Maine retreats to sunlit deserts, tropical islands, and historic European villas.

Often compared to a modern Miss Marple with champagne, the series blends traditional puzzle-solving, gentle humor, and richly drawn settings for readers who enjoy classic whodunits with a strong sense of place.

A lifelong landscape painter, Jennifer brings an artist's eye to every setting. She lives in Northwest Georgia with her husband, their sons, and two adventurous dogs. Discover more Ms. Mia Murder Mysteries, exclusive art, and behind-the-scenes insights at www.JenniferBranch.com.